Derby Scribes 2011

www.derbyscribes.

ISBN: 978-0-9530016-1-3

Published by Stumar Press 2011.

Stumar Press

www.stumarpress.co.uk

Copyright 2011. All rights belong to the original authors and artists for their contributed works. All rights reserved. Featuring an introduction by Alex Davis, short stories from Derby Scribes members Alison J. Hill, Christopher Barker, David Ball, Jennifer Brown, Peter Borg, Richard Farren Barber, Stuart Hughes and Victoria Charvill, plus guest authors Conrad Williams, Neal James and Simon Clark. Art work by Samantha Eynon.

The Gallery by Conrad Williams was first published in *The Third Alternative*, issue 15 (1998); *Brylcreem and Pipe Tobacco* by Stuart Hughes was first published online in *Golden Visions Magazine*, issue 14 (2011); all other stories are published here for the first time.

This book is a work of fiction. All characters, names, places and incidents portrayed in this book are either the product of the author's imagination or used fictitiously, and any resemblance to real people or events is purely coincidental.

This book is sold subject to the condition that it shall not, by way of trade or otherwise, be lent, re-sold, hired out, reproduced, scanned or distributed in any form, including digital and electronic or mechanical, including photocopying, recording, or by any information storage and retrieval system, without the prior written consent of the publisher, or otherwise circulated in any form of binding or cover other than that in which this is published and without a similar condition including this condition being imposed on the subsequent purchaser.

First published in 2011 by Stumar Press.

ISBN: 978-0-9530016-1-3

Contents

Introduction by Alex Davis — 5

In the Spirit of Darwin by Simon Clark — 7

Brylcreem and Pipe Tobacco by Stuart Hughes — 16

Stump by Victoria Charvill — 25

Leaving Jessica by Jennifer Brown — 28

Last Respects by Richard Farren Barber — 38

The Wake Up Call by Alison J. Hill — 45

The Gallery by Conrad Williams — 53

Dave's Dinosaur by Peter Borg — 76

An Interstellar Taxi Ride by David Ball — 79

Obsolete by Christopher Barker — 85

The Smell of Fear by Neal James — 100

Biographies — 105

Introduction
Alex Davis

I must admit it was a great pleasure to be asked to write this introduction, having had a years-long involvement in the group that would eventually become Derby Scribes. Back in 2004 I set up a group called 'Sepulchre', devoted to the darker side of writing (and a name probably inspired by too much Edgar Allan Poe as a youngster). For me it was trying to create something different to many of the groups I had been to around the time, where I felt my own horror writing didn't quite fit. And luckily enough it managed to draw together a group of like-minded people and achieve that aim.

Unfortunately I couldn't keep up Sepulchre forever, and as the workload gradually crept up I had to hand over the reins of the group, and at this point the group became Derby Scribes, which I suspect is a far more sensible name for a writing group.

It's been great to see over many years that, while the ownership may have changed a few times, the group has remained strong and the membership has remained loyal and consistent. On a personal level, I met a lot of my friends through the group, not to mention my wife, so it's played a big part in my life beyond writing as well!

As for the anthology itself, it's an exciting mixture of quality emerging writers as well as some great established names. Simon Clark's unorthodox tale of an extraordinary meeting of two historical heroes, Conrad Williams's story of reading as the darkest kind of crime in an oppressive society and Neal James's concluding piece of territorial battling all add a tasty layer of icing to what is already a pretty damn fine cake. All of these writers have attended and supported Scribes down the years, so it's great to see them continuing that association.

The current members of Scribes have a great chance to shine here as well, with a wide variety of stories, from the relative innocence of Victoria Charvill's *Stump* to the much darker recesses of Richard Farren Barber's poignant *Last Respects* and the surreal and otherworldly quality of Christopher Barker's *Obsolete*. Couple that with the supernatural overtones of Stuart Hughes's *Brylcreem and Pipe Tobacco*, a shady story of attempting to escape your own past in Jennifer Brown's *Leaving Jessica* and the twist in the tale of Alison J. Hill's *The Wake Up Call*, and you have a collection that amply demonstrates the roots of Scribes as something a bit darker than your typical writing group.

But there are some great moments of light, and humour, as well. The absurd future envisaged in David Ball's *An Interstellar Taxi Ride* and the wry smile that permeates with Peter Borg's *Dave's Dinosaur* lift the mood expertly, adding another side to the collection. Overall it's a versatile and multi-faceted anthology, blending corners of reality with aspects of the fantastical in a refreshing way.

So enjoy the stories, and – if you can – get yourself down to Derby Scribes and meet the gang. It's friendly, helpful, encouraging and useful. And as for the standard of writing? Well, in 100 pages or so, you won't need me to tell you just how good that is.

Alex Davis

Founder, Derby Scribes (formerly Sepulchre)

In the Spirit of Darwin
Simon Clark

Mister Lloyd Jefferson met Sir Charles Darwin in Badsworth Country park on the 26th May, 2010. Lloyd had celebrated his eighty-fourth birthday at the beginning of the week, and he'd decided that he'd reached an age when he feared nothing and nobody. More than ever in life, he derived satisfaction from being part of the world, moving through its landscapes, hearing the sounds, enjoying the sights, and deriving great pleasure from the warm sunshine on his face.

"Good afternoon, Mr. Jefferson. My name is Darwin." The young man lowered his head in a courteous bow. His thinning blonde hair gifted him a broad, smooth forehead. His features were pleasant. While his large, expressive eyes suggested they had the capacity to be, from time to time, quite melancholy.

"Good afternoon. Lovely day, isn't it?" Lloyd peered at the young man. "I'm sorry I can't quite place you. Are you Keith Darwin's son? From the pizza takeaway?"

"No, sir." The contrast between the soulful eyes and smiling lips could tug many a heartstring. "Charles Darwin. Sir Charles Darwin. I don't like to use the title. It makes one appear snooty."

"Oh?"

"Please don't go. I came here with the express purpose of speaking with you."

"I'm flattered. However, you appreciate my dilemma?"

"And that is?"

"If I have a conversation with Sir Charles Darwin, I'll be talking to someone who's been dead for..." He hazarded a guess. "One hundred and twenty years."

"Almost one hundred and thirty. Charles Robert Darwin, born

1809, departed this earth 1882."

"Oh."

"Honoured, sir." The young man held out his hand.

Lloyd took in the man's appearance, other than the fair, wispy hair and melancholy eyes, which he'd already noted. The stranger was clean-shaven. Well-groomed. He wore a long coat in pale, brown wool; the garment possessed the widest lapels Lloyd had ever seen. Nobody else was in sight on this woodland path. Apart from birds in the trees overhead, they were quite alone.

Then I am eighty-four, thought Lloyd, *afraid of no-one and nothing.*

He shook the man's hand. "Good afternoon, Sir Charles Darwin." What harm could it do, accepting the man's statement at face-value?

"Pleased to meet you, sir. But please use the name Darwin."

"Then call me Lloyd."

"Indeed I will, sir." He smiled. "Delighted to make your acquaintance, Lloyd."

"What can I do for you, Darwin?"

"I'd like the opportunity to speak with you."

"By all means."

"However, my appearance perplexes you?"

Lloyd thought for a moment. "I don't intend to be impolite, but I recall photographs that show you to be balding with a long, white beard."

"Indeed, later in life the bald pate and extravagant beard were there. However, I was granted the opportunity to make my appearance here as I looked as a thirty-year old. Vanity prevailed. Hence my youthful face."

"I'm eighty-four, so don't have many pressing engagements."

"So you will consent to chat with me as we walk?" Darwin was delighted.

"Why not?"

"Such a lovely day. Why not make the most of it?"

They continued along the woodland path. Birds sang. Rabbits hopped through the long grass.

"I'm continuing my work," Darwin told him.

"The study of evolution?"

"Yes, but at the risk of sounding flippant, my interests are evolving, too."

"Oh?"

"I'm now studying the evolution of the human mind."

"Sounds complicated."

"It can be. However, many aspects of the human mind are more straightforward than you might think."

"Do you collect specimens?"

"Of mind?"

"Hardly." Lloyd smiled. "Human behaviour, I meant."

Darwin produced a camera from his coat pocket. "This records video as well as still images. I film what people do, and how they react to stimuli."

"You know about digital movie cameras?"

"My body might have been laid to rest in 1882, but I'm not so out of touch with the world. For example, I drove to this park in a Ford Focus."

"So why the interest in human behaviour?"

"The evolution of the mind is key to humanity's survival, or possibly the reason for its extinction. Only time will tell."

"Does modern human behaviour instil optimism?"

"To a degree."

"All the wars, the race riots, the bigotry, the envy, the greed? The naked pursuit of power, whether masked by religious faith, or a pretence that it's for the common good?"

"That does sound like pessimism, Lloyd."

"Eighty-four years of life does that. You constantly have your nose rubbed in life's grubby realities. For example, football fans from another town smashed up shops in my local high street a few weeks ago. Innocent people were attacked."

"You're not a football fan, Lloyd?"

"I'm not a fan of a sport that encourages xenophobia, or hostility to the supporters of other teams, simply because they are fans of that other team."

"Surely, such hostility isn't officially endorsed by football clubs?"

"Obviously not, Darwin. But there is a certain fascism that attaches itself to the world of football. Generally speaking, society deems it compulsory for every man to support a football team. If a man should even dare to admit not being interested in football then he is likely to be considered strange. Work colleagues will be suspicious. He'll no longer be part of the male fraternity. Once he becomes an outsider he may be treated with contempt, passed over for promotion, or physically attacked."

Darwin nodded. "What drives the passion for football and team games is an instinct that evolved when humans were hunter gatherers. The popular image is of hunters leaving the village to hunt antelope, for example, in a single group. What actually happened was that at least two teams of hunters would go in search of game. The first to make the kill and bring it back to the village were celebrated as victors. The winning team members also won the hearts of the girls. Consequently, the winners' DNA survived in the offspring; hence, a competitive nature became inbred."

"Does that competitive urge have a place in modern society?"

"To a degree. In fact, there are many vestigial instincts that continue to influence behaviour. Just as you find the remains of obsolete organs, such as gills in your neck, or tiny obsolete legs on certain species of snake, so ancient psychological features still exist inside our heads."

Lloyd spoke with some hostility, "You're telling me that prejudice, fascism, and racial discrimination are the natural order of things? That it's okay to make jokes about men and women with red hair? Or discriminate against people, because society doesn't favour a certain body shape?"

"These instincts, unpalatable though they are, did play their part in human evolution."

"If so, that's unforgivable."

"Lloyd. Human beings would, as a matter of course, defecate in public. If they were hungry, they would tear food from the hands of juvenile members of their tribe. That doesn't happen now. Humans evolve. We don't hunt with spears. We don't have to yield to prejudice."

"You really believe that bigots can stop themselves hating people with different coloured skins?"

"What happened when you were thirteen years old, Lloyd?"

"That's seventy-one years ago. You expect me to remember?"

"Oh, you remember the incident well."

"What incident?"

"The Sunday you and your friends went to the house in Mafeking Terrace. A gentleman was repairing a bicycle tyre in his back yard. He wore an orange turban. The colliery brass band was playing hymns in the park nearby."

"How can you know about that?" Lloyd stared at the man. "Who told you?"

"Just as I've been permitted to come here and speak with you so I've been permitted a glimpse into your past."

Lloyd's heart pounded. "I don't know who put you up to this, but leave me alone!"

"Why?"

"You know why?"

"Because of what you did to the man in the orange turban?"

"Go away!"

"I do want to discuss something of importance, Lloyd."

"I tolerated you because I thought you were harmless. Now I can see you want to torment an old man!"

"But you are a remarkable man."

"I'm nothing of the sort."

"You are. You are remarkable, because you changed what you believed in."

"Please, stop..." Lloyd walked faster along the path. The breeze shook the trees, making the leaves hiss louder and louder, until a great whooshing moved through the forest.

Darwin followed. "On that Sunday you learned that an Indian gentlemen had moved into Mafeking Terrace. You and your friends went to see what he looked like, because Asian immigrants were rare in the town."

"Stop it."

"Firstly, you called him names. When that didn't provoke him sufficiently, you began throwing stones. One you threw almost hit the gentleman in the face. He flinched, lost his balance, and fell backwards onto his rear. You and your friends ran away. They were all laughing. You laughed the loudest."

"Okay, so you heard what I did. That kind of behaviour is vile."

"The Sikh gentleman wasn't hurt."

"How do *you* know?"

"Oh, I know, Lloyd."

"So, you exposed me, Darwin – if that's your real name. I'm a bigot."

"No, you're not. A spider must always be like its spider ancestors, unless modified by natural selection. Human beings, however, have the power to change their minds. They can modify their behaviour."

"Why torment me, young man?"

"I'm not tormenting you. What you did to the Sikh gentleman was deeply unpleasant. As was the occasion you teased an overweight boy at school, calling him 'Fatty' and 'Piggy'."

"Dear God, how can you know all this about me?"

"But this is the important fact." Darwin held up his finger to emphasise the point. "By the time you were eighteen years of age you realised what you did was wrong. You despised the way you once considered overweight people to be figures of fun, or for people of different coloured skin to be inferior. Nobody taught this to you, did they? A spirit did not appear and tell you that racial prejudice is wrong?"

Lloyd shook his head.

Darwin continued. "You gradually reached that understanding yourself. To rectify what you believe, without being ordered or cajoled, is quite an achievement."

"I gather I'm supposed to learn something profound from this encounter with you?" Lloyd walked on – weary now. Drained by this raking up of his past.

"On the contrary. I want to learn from you."

"How will you do that?"

"You asked earlier if I collected minds as specimens."

"I was being whimsical."

"Well, Lloyd, I wish to collect yours."

"You want my mind? Ha, to stick it in a jar full of spirit to preserve it, no doubt?"

"Yes. At least figuratively speaking."

"Young man, this has been entertaining... and at times harrowing, but I think our meeting is over." Lloyd walked faster along the woodland path. Somewhere he'd found a reserve of energy; his feet seemed much lighter than before. His heart no longer hammered like some rusty, old motor.

Darwin followed. "I've been given permission to collect valuable specimens. I want you to consent to helping me with my research."

"You've been given permission by God, I suppose."

"No. This is an assembly of life forms that are benevolent, and as natural as grass, cats and butterflies."

"How charmingly imaginative."

"So, I am collecting minds that have special qualities."

"You intend to kill me? Go on then, how can I stop you?"

"No. I will collect the mind at the moment of your natural death."

"That's merciful, at least."

"So you consent?"

"Why not? Harvest my thoughts, memories and such, when the time comes."

"You are humouring me, Lloyd."

"Apologies. But I do need to get back home to hang out my washing."

They cut down a path that lead toward the car park.

Darwin said, "I have your word, then, that I might collect your mind at the moment of death?"

"Of course. Now I'll have to say goodbye."

"I should explain: there is a specimen jar waiting for you — of sorts — and filled with a spirit — of sorts."

"This spirit of yours, will it hurt me?"

"There'll be no pain."

"Surely, it will be heartless to leave me suspended in some stuff or other for all eternity?"

"I promise, there'll be no discomfort, no loneliness. Whenever you wish, we can accommodate you in another body. You can then walk the earth for another eight decades, or so."

"Will I have friends in this place of yours?"

Darwin's soulful eyes regarded him. "You do have friends. And they are waiting for you now. All you need do is close your eyes. When you open them again you will see smiling faces."

Lloyd headed toward the parked cars. "I'll have to pinch myself. I'm starting to believe this fantasy of yours." He smiled. "But if you do intend to wait for me to pop off, so to speak, you might be waiting for a long time. I feel fit as a fiddle."

"Well, Lloyd. Actually, the time is now." He pointed. "Don't you recognise the man lying on the park bench?" He gave a kindly smile. "You've seen his face many times before in the mirror."

"Ah..." Lloyd sighed as, at last, he understood. "Not a bad exit, is it? On a warm, sunny day with four and eighty years behind me."

"Lloyd. It's time to close your eyes."

Mister Lloyd Jefferson did so. And there he was: safe in the spirit of Darwin.

Brylcreem and Pipe Tobacco
Stuart Hughes

"That's it," Claire said, pointing. She looked across at Rodney as he eased the Jaguar to a stop.

Rodney turned to face her. "Are you sure you want to go through with this?" he asked. "Absolutely certain?"

Claire was certain. She loved Rodney, despite his faults. She wanted to marry him – as soon as possible – but she loved Charlie too, and she couldn't possibly marry Rodney without Charlie's blessing.

"Yes," she said in answer to Rodney's question. The word was nothing more than a whisper.

Rodney sighed and stared through the windscreen.

Claire pulled the visor down and looked at herself in the mirror. Despite her fifty-two years of age, her face was remarkably smooth and unblemished. Her grey hair – since Charlie died she had stopped dying it brunette – was swept back and tied in a harsh bun. Satisfied that there were no loose strands to attend to, Claire flipped the visor back up.

Rodney had fished the card out of his pocket and was staring at it. "This is crazy!" he exclaimed. "Do you know what this says?"

Claire did know but she said nothing.

Rodney read the card aloud and Claire couldn't miss the sarcasm in his voice:

JUST A HUNCH! NOBODY BELIEVES YOU!

TRY – SIDRICK RODRIGUES

Mystic-Soothsayer-Oracle Mysteries of the Occult revealed.

Consultation *by Appointment Only.*

When he'd finished reading, Rodney screwed the card into a ball, and tossed it onto the back seat. "You don't have to go through with this," he said. "I can drive you home, right now."

"I have to," Claire said.

"Are you sure?" he asked. A long strand of grey hair fell down over his brown marble-like eyes and he brushed it back. "It's crazy. Absolutely crazy!"

"I know," Claire said. She couldn't expect him to understand. Rodney was a big name on the local council, but all his contacts were in this world, the real world, and in this world, Rodney's world, there was no room for ghosts or spirits. But Claire knew better. There were times when she could feel Charlie's presence and knew he was close. Sometimes she could smell his pipe tobacco or the brylcreem he always slicked his hair back with, and once she had even heard his voice whispering in the breeze. She knew Charlie was with her, watching out for her, but Claire couldn't tell Rodney that. He wouldn't understand. "I know you mean well," she told him instead, "but this is something I *have* to do."

Rodney remained silent.

"Humour me tonight, dear. Please."

"All right," Rodney said and shrugged. "I give up." He looked at her and attempted a smile that didn't quite sit right on his face. Claire appreciated the effort. "But I'm coming with you."

Claire smiled and patted his thigh. "Thank you," she said. "I'd like that."

Claire rang the door bell.

"Promise me you won't lose your temper tonight, dear."

Rodney shrugged but didn't answer. He was a big man and Claire had long ago given up trying to talk him into exercising or – God forbid – going on a diet. Today he was wearing a light brown suit, white shirt, dark brown tie, and a dark brown waistcoat that creased in all the wrong places across his pot belly. His shoes were dark brown too and polished to perfection. Brown was his favourite colour, and the contents of his wardrobe reflected that, but Claire didn't mind because it complemented his brown marble-like eyes.

Llewellyn, the butler, opened the door. His hair was silvery, parted down the middle, and slicked back in a typically Victorian style. Llewellyn seemed to smile, although the thick white moustache on his upper lip made it difficult to tell for sure.

"Good evening, Mrs. Webster," Llewellyn said. "So nice to see you again. Good evening, Sir. Please do come in."

They stepped inside. The hallway was plain and uncarpeted. There was a heavy oak door to both left and right, and further down the hall was a sliding door. In front of them rose a wide, beautifully polished staircase.

Llewellyn closed the door with slow, rather laboured movements. "Mr. Rodrigues is expecting you," he said. "Would you follow me please?" He led the way down the hall and opened the sliding door.

As they entered the room, Rodrigues rose, rounded the large desk, nodded his head towards Claire, then turned towards Rodney and extended his hand. "Good evening, Mrs. Webster, Mr. Stevenson."

Rodney declined to shake hands as Claire knew he would. She watched Rodrigues' face, as he casually dropped the offered hand into the trouser pocket of his white suit, but it didn't flicker with surprise, or embarrassment, or anything...

"You know my name?" Rodney said. He sounded surprised.

"Of course," Rodrigues said.

"You've clearly done your homework, Mr. Rodrigues," Rodney said.

"I can assure you that I have done no such thing. I can read everything I need to know in your eyes, Mr. Stevenson, and see it in your face. Your face tells me much." Rodrigues smiled, revealing two rows of perfect white teeth.

Rodney laughed. "You won't fool me that easily."

Claire moved to Rodney's side, slipped her arm around his waist, and lightly pecked his cheek. "You said you'd humour me tonight, dear."

"All right," Rodney said but his steely gaze never wavered from Rodrigues. "But I promise you, Rodrigues, if I get so much as a sniff of any illegal jiggery pokery going on here, I'll have the police down on you so fast, you–"

"Rodney, please."

He fell silent.

"Thank you, Mrs. Webster," Rodrigues said. "Can I get you both a drink? Coffee? Something stronger perhaps?"

"Let's just get this damned business over and done with," Rodney said.

Rodrigues glanced towards Claire. She nodded. Rodney wasn't going to believe until he had seen for himself.

"Very well," Rodrigues said. "Will you follow me please?"

The room was already prepared. Curtains drawn. A round table stood in the centre surrounded by four chairs. The rest of the room was empty, except for a chandelier hanging directly above the table. Rodrigues gestured towards the chairs. "Mrs. Webster, Mr. Stevenson, you will sit opposite each other please."

Claire placed her handbag on the table and allowed Rodrigues to help her sit down. Rodney hadn't moved. "Take a seat, dear," she said. "It won't bite."

Rodney sat down opposite her, clearly reluctant. His face looked like thunder.

Rodrigues settled himself into one of the two vacant chairs, then asked, "Did you bring those items I requested?"

"Yes," Claire said, her voice trembling slightly. She always got nervous once the proceedings were under way, whether it was the Tarot cards, or the Ouija board, or a full blown séance. Tonight she was doubly nervous because the rest of her life hung on Charlie's answer.

She rummaged inside her handbag for a moment, then took out a white envelope with her right hand.

"Good," Rodrigues said. "Will you place them in the centre of the table please? The photograph of your husband first, face up, and his wedding ring on top."

Claire untucked the flap, turned the envelope upside down, and allowed the gold ring to fall out into her left hand. The photo was stuck, so she pulled it out with trembling fingers. She placed the objects exactly as Rodrigues had instructed. The photo showed a youthful Charlie on their wedding day, hair slicked back with brylcreem, wearing a morning suit, and a top hat tucked under his arm. The photo was black and white, somewhat faded with age, and didn't do justice to Charlie's most striking feature – his brilliant blue eyes. The ring was 22 carat.

"Thank you, Mrs. Webster." Rodrigues leant forward and placed his palms flat on the table. "Lights please, Llewellyn."

The room plunged into darkness. Claire heard Llewellyn shuffle to the table, scrape the last remaining chair back, sit down, and then there was no sound at all.

Not an eerie silence.

Just silence.

Rodrigues spoke first: "I would like you all to place your hands flat on the table, fingers splayed so that they touch the fingers of the person next to you."

The table was cold to her touch. Claire spread her fingers and felt them touch Rodrigues' fingers to the left and Llewellyn's to her right.

"Good," Rodrigues continued. "Now we will take some deep breaths and relax. You may close your eyes, or keep them open, whichever feels the most comfortable." His tone of voice was different now, slower, each word – no, *every* syllable – more pronounced.

"Just relax," his voice went on, soothing Claire, helping her relax with every deep breath. "Relax, that's the important thing, relax, relax..."

Her eyes were getting accustomed to the gloom now. Rodrigues' head was tilted back so that his face was pointing towards the ceiling, the muscles in his neck standing taut in cords. As she watched, Rodrigues began to speak in that flat monotone again: "Charlie... Charlie... Webster. There is someone here who wants to speak to you."

Nothing happened.

"Charlie, your beloved wife Claire is here. She wants to talk to you."

Nothing happened.

Claire was mesmerised. She stared at Rodrigues and waited, expectantly. His voice had sunk to a low mumble. His head tilted to one side, beads of sweat breaking out on his brow, lines of concentration etched across his forehead.

And still nothing happened, although Claire thought she could make out a faint smell of brylcreem and Charlie's favourite tobacco.

Then the temperature dropped.

Claire shivered.

The smell of brylcreem got stronger.

And the aroma of Charlie's favourite tobacco.

"Charlie, you are close now." Rodrigues' voice was barely audible. "I can sense you, Charlie. Claire is anxious to talk to you. Will you make your presence known to us?"

Claire wondered if Rodney had noticed the drop in temperature and looked across the table at him. But she could hardly see him. His face was hazy, as if a patch of fog was sitting on the table between them.

"Charlie..." Rodrigues' head rolled slowly from shoulder to

shoulder. "We are your friends, Charlie. We don't mean you any harm. Claire loves you, Charlie. She wants your blessing. Please... Charlie... make yourself known to us."

She tried to watch Rodrigues but her gaze was constantly drawn to the photograph of Charlie, sitting in the centre of the table with the gold wedding ring on top of it. The photograph started to glow: first white, then yellow, orange, red... and then it burst into flames.

Claire gasped.

Blue flames rose from the photograph, swirling upwards. The photo curled at the edges, then shrivelled away to nothing beneath the wedding ring. The flames continued to rise though, higher and higher, leaping and dancing, upwards, enchanting and beautiful.

Claire stared. The flames were hovering now at head height, flickering, sparking, then the flames began to take definition, to form a shape – no, a face.

At first Claire could only vaguely make out the shape of the face. There were three hollows in the flickering flames for the eyes and mouth and there was a protrusion that had to be the nose. Then the flames became more defined and she recognised the face floating above the table.

"Charlie," she said excitedly. "Is it you, Charlie?"

"Poppycock!" Rodney exclaimed. He pushed his chair back and it scraped across the floor. "This is complete and utter poppycock. I'm not fooled by these cheap parlour tricks."

He leant forward over the table and swept his arm through Charlie's face. There was a high pitched buzzing, that sounded like electricity, but the arc of his swing through the flickering flames was unimpeded as if there was nothing there at all. Charlie's face faded for a moment before disappearing completely.

"Come on, Claire," Rodney said. "Let's go." He didn't wait for a response, simply turned his back and marched purposefully out of the room.

Claire was too stunned to speak. Rodrigues and Llewellyn said nothing, taking their lead from her. Eventually Claire gathered her composure and wiped her eyes with the back of her hand.

"I'm sorry," she said, her voice cracking. "It was a mistake to bring him here." She grabbed her handbag, opened it, and took out her purse.

"No," Rodrigues said. He flicked his hand dismissively and moved around the table, holding Claire's chair for her as she got to her feet.

Llewellyn switched on the lights and Claire blinked a few times against the sudden brightness.

"I'm so sorry," Claire said. She picked up the wedding ring and put it in her purse.

"Don't be," Rodrigues said.

Claire nodded and then she hurried from the room.

Rodney was standing on the drive just outside the front door, facing away from the house, his hands stuffed in his trouser pockets, his head bowed.

Claire paid him no attention as she hurried past and walked briskly towards the Jaguar. She stood by the passenger door and waited, without once looking back at Rodney. There was a bleep, amber lights flashed, and Claire opened the passenger door, climbed inside and, with all the mental determination she could muster, resisted the urge to slam the car door, closing it very carefully instead.

She put her handbag between her feet in the foot well and was fastening her seat belt when the driver's door opened. She resisted the temptation to look across at Rodney as he climbed in beside her.

Neither of them spoke. Claire wasn't sure how she felt at that moment, probably a combination of anger, resentment and frustration. Disappointment was right up there too, she thought. She was disappointed in Rodney. Bitterly disappointed.

"Poppycock," Rodney said quietly. Claire wasn't sure if he was talking to her or to himself. "Poppycock," he said again, a bit louder this time, and laughed in a way she had never heard him laugh before, a gleeful cackle that was totally out of character but somehow familiar nevertheless.

"Well, that was an interesting evening," Rodney said.

"I don't understand you at times," Claire said, with a little more venom in her voice than she'd actually intended.

"What did I do?"

"You know very well," Claire said, still stubbornly refusing to look at him. "You said you'd humour me tonight... but, instead of that, you *humiliated* me." She could feel tears forming in the corner of her eyes and wiped them away. "You ruined *everything*."

"No I didn't," Rodney said.

"It was a mistake," Claire allowed her voice to trail off and finished the sentence in her mind only, *to bring you here tonight*.

Tears formed in her eyes again and this time she let them flow down her cheeks.

"You don't need Charlie's blessing," Rodney said and reached over and patted her knee, then he stroked her upper arm in a way he'd never done before... but the caress was very familiar. Charlie had often stroked her like that when she was upset.

Claire finally turned her head and looked at Rodney through tear streaked eyes. Her vision was blurry but, despite the blurriness, she could see him watching her with brilliant blue eyes.

"You don't need Charlie's blessing any more," he said and smiled at her, "because I'm here now."

Was that brylcreem and pipe tobacco she could smell or was that just her imagination?

He pressed a button on the dashboard and locked the car doors.

"Will you marry me, Claire?" he asked. "Will you marry me *again*?"

Stump
Victoria Charvill

Sophie had named the guinea pig Stump, just in case. As much as she loved animals, hers never seemed to last long.

Her tortoise, Milly, had somehow found its way to the top branches of the oak in their garden. How it got there was a mystery, but it wasn't found until it fell on top of Kelly, the family's Yorkshire Terrier. After that incident, her parents bought her some goldfish, which kept jumping out of the tank onto Sophie's bed. Somehow they thought that Sophie wanted to take them into bed with her to keep them warm. Luckily for Sophie, her great-aunt Joyce came over to stay. Sophie was made to sleep on the sofa bed in the spare room; the sofa bed was no good for poor Aunt Joyce's hip. Then, neither was being woken up at three in the morning by a fish landing on her face.

It was Great-Aunt Joyce who decided that she should have a pet she could keep in the shed. Their shed had plenty of room for a guinea pig or two to have a hutch. A guinea pig would be best for Sophie. It could have a run built in the garden as well as being nice and safe in the shed at night. There was no way a guinea pig could get itself stuck up the tree when it was enclosed all the time. More importantly, guinea pigs do not jump on people at three in the morning.

Her father set to work building the hutch and enclosure within the family's shed, closely observed by Sophie.

"Daddy?" asked Sophie. "Will the guinea pig be able to climb and get stuck inside the grass chopper?"

"No, sweetheart, the guinea pig won't be able to climb over the partition, so there is no way it can get stuck inside the lawn mower."

"But, Daddy, that fence is smaller than me, and I am only little yet."

"I know, but guinea pigs are even smaller than you. It is very large for a guinea pig."

Sophie frowned at her father. "But if he *does* escape, there are all your tools in here. Ones I am not allowed to go near, so they must be ever so bad for a guinea pig."

Her father put down his hammer, wiped his hands on his trousers and knelt in front of Sophie. His kind eyes level with hers.

"I promise you, the guinea pig will not be able to escape and will never get near any of my tools." He gently pinched her nose. "Okay?"

"I s'pose."

It was then her mother returned with her guinea pig. It had been put into its run until the area in the shed was complete. Sophie peered at the creature, at its ginger hair and white crown, waiting for it to move away from the door so she could throw in a carrot before it escaped. She thought about all the sharp tools her father kept in the shed.

"Stump. That's what I'll call you. Just in case."

That night, a storm raged outside. The old oak tree could not stand its ground against the gale. As it fell, it met the shed. Sophie was woken up by the loud splintering sound, and sought the warmth and safety of her parents' bed. She'd never liked storms.

When she did see what had happened, she dragged her parents up, forcing them to go and check whether or not Stump was okay. Her father searched the remains of the shed, whilst her mother looked around the garden. There was no sign of Stump.

Sophie nodded as her parents told her.

"I know," she rolled her eyes. "I shouldn't have any more pets. I don't want you to get me any more."

She looked out at the garden, the branches and trunk had crashed through the middle of the shed. The jagged wood of the trunk showed where the tree had snapped. Sophie caught a glimpse of ginger fur move in the hollow.

"Look!" she pointed.

Her father wandered over and returned with Stump.

"Looks like you chose the right name for him after all."

He squeaked happily as her father placed him in Sophie's arms.

Leaving Jessica
Jennifer Brown

Jessica Athleston died on Monday, September 24th.

It happened the moment I glanced out of the window to check on Sally. Sally had been playing shop on the front lawn in the late afternoon sun with her teddy bear and her toy cash register, her establishment's boundaries marked by the edges of the checked blanket laid down within full view of the kitchen window, where I was washing up. Seeing her frozen and quiet in mid-play as she stared across the street, I knew what had spooked her before I'd even followed her gaze.

Sure enough, on the other side of the road, underneath the oak tree outside Mrs. Freeman's house, there was parked a black Audi estate, the driver watching Sally patiently. I didn't know how long he'd been there but I knew *why* he was there.

Probably armed, he was waiting for me.

My heart sank and the lump forming in my throat made me suddenly realise how much I loved Jessica and her quiet little nanny's life, and I blinked away a tear. "Time to go," I stated quietly, as business-like as I could manage.

The driver's gaze shifted suddenly, landing straight on the kitchen window and I gasped and jumped back, freezing. Just a moment later the car door opened and the driver began to get out. My eyes darted between him and Sally, my first thought being getting her inside to safety, but I had no idea how to do that without making both of us vulnerable. Sally was still staring at him warily as he began to cross the road towards the house and I silently begged her to lose her nerve and come running in. She didn't.

When I couldn't wait any longer, I made a dash for the door but, just as I yanked it open, salvation arrived. Sally's mother's car appeared around the corner, indicating, and turning into the driveway. The man from the Audi smoothly changed course and kept his eyes down as he pretended to be heading up the street.

For the moment, I was safe, and I let out a breath I didn't know I'd been holding.

As I relaxed, Sally's mum opened her door and got out, turning towards the grass and holding her arms wide for hugs from her daughter. "Sally, I'm home!"

All pre-occupation with the strange man suddenly left the child and, beaming, she waddled across the garden at top speed. She hadn't been walking all that long. I hadn't known her to be crawling all that long either, truth be told. How they'd found me so quickly, I didn't know.

I held back more tears as I grabbed a dish cloth and dried my hands off, schooling my features, turning towards Fiona as she bustled in with Sally in her arms, to toss her car keys onto the table.

"Hi, Jessica." I was greeted cheerily. "How are things?"

"Fine," I answered. "Dinner's in the oven."

"Great." I must have had a few tell-tale signs of upset on my face because Fiona paused, a look of curious concern in her eyes. "Are you all right?"

I smiled brightly. "Of course!"

"Hmmn." She accepted it. I knew she'd noticed the sadness that came and went with my introspection, she was used to it, and she'd got very early on that I wasn't one to discuss my feelings too much. She left the kitchen still carrying Sally and I heard the television come on and Fiona enquire as to the day's activities.

With another sigh, I turned back to the window and stared at the Audi, the driver back behind the wheel. He couldn't stay there forever; with Fiona now home and her husband Michael due back in the next half hour or so, his position was becoming risky and I could easily stay inside until he had gone. Maybe he hadn't confirmed it, but he knew I was in here. He could try again. I knew how they worked, they'd found me before. How many times had it been now?

I counted them off on my fingers. Eight lives. And now the ninth was gone. I hoped I'd get more than the proverbial cat.

A rising apprehension making my insides twist, I quietly hurried upstairs, shut and locked my bedroom door behind me, and phoned the only constant I'd had for the last nine years. He picked up on the third ring.

"Hello?" came the familiar gravelly voice, ravaged by cigarettes.

"Moxy, it's Hannah."

"Hannah? Found you again, have they?"

I nodded even though he couldn't see, tears suddenly welling in my eyes. "Can you help me?"

"Of course." Sympathy was thick in his voice. "I'll get started right away. I'll have you a new name in no time. Don't worry yourself. Where are you?"

I told him and he said, "Oh," surprised. "I've had to move, myself. The police were sniffing. I'm not far from you. Find yourself a hotel, let me know where, and when everything's ready, I'll bring it. You know the drill."

Michael's return was announced with the slamming of a car door as dusk was just about setting in.

"Did you hear that?" I asked Sally as I tucked the bedclothes in around her. "Daddy's home."

She grinned. "Daddy!"

Sally didn't attempt to escape from her bed or shout for him or anything you might expect, but that was because she was fully assured that he'd come up to see her. He did just that, coming into the bedroom as I was pulling a storybook from the shelf. It was an anthology, containing the story she'd never tire of and would have heard far more if only I hadn't got so sick of it.

"Hi." I smiled weakly as he greeted me briefly before descending on his daughter.

"How's my girl?" he asked, leaning over her and scrubbing her hair with his knuckles. "What did you do today?"

She didn't answer, still needing prompting as most small children did, so I obliged. "Tell Daddy what we did today."

"Li– library."

"Library?" he exclaimed, delighted for her in that false manner that kids never picked up on.

"We went to story-time at the library," I supplied. "We had a story all about a crocodile."

"A crocodile. Wow." Michael made a show of being impressed and Sally drank it up.

I tapped the book against my hand. "Do you want to read to her tonight? I'm..."

"Oh."

I always read the story on a weekday; he seemed a little taken aback.

"Sure," he agreed, not exactly averse to the idea and apparently not too concerned that I was slacking off. "Sure. What are we reading?"

I left them to their tales of six little boys and six little girls and six little dogs as cool as cucumbers and made my way quietly downstairs to serve up dinner.

About half way through the main course Michael shook me out of my silent mental planning when he spoke.

"You're quiet today, Jess. Everything ok?"

I leaned back in my chair and finished my mouthful of pasta bake. "Yeah, not bad."

"We've got a new secretary at work, she looks just like you."

"Oh, really?"

"Yeah. Same face, same sort of style."

I smiled sardonically. "I'm not sure I like there being another me. I'll have to try to be someone else tomorrow."

Fiona made a noise of amusement. "I've tried that on numerous occasions. The in-laws still spot me."

The rest of dinner passed with small talk and a conversation about the work being done on the bathroom the next week and I stayed mainly out of it. I listened, I paid attention, but I didn't really join in. I didn't really have a place there anymore.

After I'd finished cleaning up I went back to my room and picked up my mobile phone, scrolling through the phonebook to my boyfriend's entry. It had been silly of me to even start seeing someone, really, but I'd been getting more and more lax.

When I first ran away, I tried literally and figuratively living out of a suitcase. I took a single rented room, kept my possessions to a bare minimum, and made sure I was ready to run at any moment. I stayed like that for a while, running through the first three new identities I had at a worrying speed, but as I got better at hiding, it took longer for them to find me each time and I started to slow down. Being temporary was wearing. So my accommodation got steadily more lived in, my jobs got steadily more permanent, and my acquaintances started becoming friends. And being Jessica, I'd finally reached a point where not only was it impractical to disappear at a moment's notice, it was also sad. I'd let myself get attached to my life.

I bit my lip as I listened to the phone ring, mumbled conversation and Fiona's news broadcast floating up from downstairs.

John picked up.

"Hi, darling! What's up?"

"Hi," I returned with fake warmth, a sick feeling in my stomach. "Listen, I'm really sorry, but I'll have to cancel tomorrow night. I need to work."

"Oh. That's a shame. Are 'the employers' going out?"

"Yeah. Michael's got a business dinner and it's one of those things where he really needs Fiona there. Presenting the good image, you know." The lie was smooth. I'd had a lot of practice over the years.

"Right. Well, I can always come over to you instead. Watch a DVD?"

"Erm..." It wouldn't happen, but he'd get suspicious, and probably hurt, if I said no. I never said no. "Sure," I finished.

And just like that I dropped things.

Probably Fiona and Michael's first clue that I was gone was when they'd realised no-one was going to answer the door when the bell rang at seven o'clock the next morning and, one of them going instead, they found the babysitter I'd ordered for them standing there. They'd have looked for me, found John's number in my phone, called him angrily to see if I was there. That would have been his first clue. And then it would have become very obvious very quickly that I'd skipped out overnight.

Whether or not it ever filtered through to my hunters so efficiently I never knew, but I'd only have known that by watching and I was never going to risk hanging around.

I'd climbed out of my window, clambered over the hedge to their neighbour's place, let myself out of their back gate, and met the taxi waiting for me three streets away. Then I'd slept on the chairs at the airport until the car rental place had opened up again the next morning, and driven away in a blue hatchback. I wasn't crying and I wasn't looking over my shoulder. I was, for the moment, non-existent.

I'd been waiting less than two days by the time Moxy turned up, knocking on my door in the cheap hotel. I spent a good long moment just eyeing him up through the peephole, satisfying myself it was him. Recognising my friend through the receded hair and additional lines on his face, I opened the door shyly.

"Hannah," he greeted me warmly. "I'm sorry."

I nodded.

"It's all here," he confirmed, placing a cardboard box on the bed and opening it to show me the forgeries. Driving licence, passport, national insurance number, job references... it would all be there and all I would need to do was find somewhere to live and send off some change of address forms. That way, not even Moxy knew where I was hiding. I picked up one of the documents and looked to see who I was now.

Anthea Greene. Who on earth was she?

Moxy watched me as I stared at my photo on my driving licence. He could see what I could feel — this time, it was not going to be easy.

"How long are you going to carry on like this?" he asked, his voice cutting the silence.

"Until my loving organised-crime-husband satisfies himself that I'm not going to talk to the police?"

"Come on, Hannah." Moxy sat heavily on the bed. "They won't let you go. We both know that. They're not just paranoid, they're proud. Nobody just ups and leaves them."

"Pride? Is that what you call it?"

"Call it whatever you want. It doesn't change the fact that you can't keep running. It's killing you already, it's obvious."

I pressed my fingers hard against my temples and squeezed my eyes shut against the headache that wouldn't go away. "I need some aspirin," I said quietly, and shut myself in the bathroom.

In there, I stared at myself in the mirror. Hannah didn't come out much anymore, just in anonymous hotel rooms and motorway escapes. She didn't own many clothes or have anything stable in her life. Her skin was dull and her hair unkempt and the circles under her eyes dark from lack of sleep. It was always a relief to stop being Hannah. It had not been a relief to stop being Jessica. But Jessica was gone now, and in a few days time I would become

Anthea Greene.

Suitably calmed, I emerged back into the main room. Moxy was leaning against the wall, waiting for me.

"I think you should meet with him," he said.

I snorted.

"No, really. He can be pretty reasonable, on a good day, and I think he was genuinely fond of you. Maybe you can call a truce. You agree to live in the open where they can keep an eye on you, they agree to leave you alone."

I began to pack my documents into my bag, carefully not thinking too closely about what I was doing and instead focusing on the absurdity of his suggestion. "You're suddenly thinking very highly of them."

"Well what else do you suggest?"

"I don't suggest anything." I pulled out the wad of bank notes I added to when I was somebody else and dipped into when I was Hannah and counted out Moxy's payment. "I'll just keep moving."

"Bad idea."

"Maybe."

He considered arguing some more but decided against it when he saw my face. Cold, closed off. Just the way I was going to stay from now on. I wasn't going to make Jessica's mistake again.

He took the money and smiled flatly. "Until we meet again."

"Yeah."

He went to leave, but paused in the open door. "Hannah? I hope it's a very long time."

His concern broke a dam, a range of held-back emotions washing over me. Almost bursting into tears again, I found myself smiling. "Me too."

Perhaps it had all been a temporary lapse. Perhaps I could still handle things.

I picked a town for my new home. As Jessica, I had lived in the suburbs of the city surrounded by Fiona and Michael's contemporaries of lawyers, doctors, accountants and businessmen. As Anthea, I thought I would go for a change of pace, and sought out somewhere near the sea.

I drew up in the hatchback near the pier, got out, and watched the cold waves crashing against the breakwaters as the tide came in. The air was salty and wet, a world away from the sheltered valley air of my previous residence. It was pleasing, bracing. It promised brisk morning walks to the corner shop in the coming winter and a following summer of tourists, crab-fishing, and boat trips to see the seals.

Across the road was one of several bed and breakfasts I'd already seen and I crossed over to it, nodding to myself at the 'Vacancies' sign outside. A bell rang as I pushed open the front door and I waited in the hallway, a reception desk built in where the wall through to the living room had been partially knocked through. The carpets were clean, the heating warm, the empty dining room visible on my left conjured up thoughts of English breakfasts. I was settling into Anthea already.

A middle-aged woman appeared from the living room and smiled widely as she came to stand at the reception.

"Hello, Madam. Can I help you?"

"Yes, I'd like a room please. I'm not sure how long for; I'm going to be staying while I look for a place to rent."

"Oh you're moving here, are you?"

"Yes. That's right."

"Single room?"

"Please."

She flipped through her reservation book, took my details, and smiled again as she dropped a key into my palm. "Room 3, up those stairs and on your left. Breakfast is between seven and nine.

Enjoy your stay, Miss Greene."

I thanked her, turned, and jogged up the stairs.

Bursting into my room, I glanced around for a mirror and, finding one, immediately ran to it and turned my back, pulling up my top and looking over my shoulder to see in my reflection the brand new eight sets of scrolled initials inked down my spine. There, at the bottom, were the letters: 'J.A.'

I smiled.

Moxy had been right, I couldn't keep running forever. Maybe I'd have to keep moving, and maybe I'd have to keep leaving friends behind, but it was silly to keep reinventing myself. Jessica Athleston had died, that was true, but Anthea Greene wasn't going to forget her.

Last Respects
Richard Farren Barber

Bryan Lamb leaned against the chalky wall, his eyes closed. Someone was whispering – either prayers or a quiet conversation, he couldn't tell which. He pretended to sleep, pretended that he couldn't hear the howitzers and feel the whole earth shake when they found their mark.

"You awake, Bry?"

"Yeah."

"Take this for Kathleen."

Bryan felt the letter pushed into his hands. He opened his eyes. The scrap of paper was already torn and dirty, the address barely legible. Pete Franklin's face was white, drained of blood and the hand which held his letter was shaking.

"You tell her yourself," Bryan said. But still he took the letter, fastened it inside his breast pocket where it would be safe. "You tell her everything in this and a lot more besides when you get back from here."

Pete was still a kid; he had lied about his age because he was taller than the rest of the boys in his school and he could get away with it. In Hucknall that had made him a man – in France it just made him a tall, scared boy.

Bryan looked at his watch – nearly seven o' clock. The air was thick with the stench of gun smoke, of munitions and death. Every second another shell screamed overhead and as it landed on the German trenches, the earth would roll. It was already light and he gave up any pretence at sleep, any hope of it. He shook himself fully awake and then cautiously stepped up onto the fire-step to look out over no-man's land.

The ground between the trenches was churned up, craters cut deep into the earth, throwing up white chalk scars. The explosions continued, if anything, louder and longer than before; surely, nothing could withstand such a pounding. Eight days they'd been at it now, eight days.

Some of the bodies in the packed trenches began to stir. Bryan didn't recognise most of the faces – fresh things, new in from the rear.

"There's thousands more of them back there," Pete said, looking to the communications trenches. "Packed in tight, waiting for a chance to move up to the front."

"Well, they can have my place," Bryan joked. His laughter was short and nervous.

Corporal Ian Harris walked the length of the section, nudging Stanwell on the shoulder with his foot, stopping to have a brief conversation with Richard Jims – a builder from Bulwell, who constantly complained he'd been allocated to the wrong platoon, that he was supposed to be Cavalry, or maybe it was Artillery, or Engineers, but definitely not Infantry.

Bryan watched Harris – they were about the same age. He didn't know how he would cope in Harris's position, wasn't sure he'd have the courage to do what was expected of a Corporal.

He checked his watch again – seven twenty – the time crawled and maybe he shouldn't be wishing it away, but surely the waiting was the worst; the sick feeling in his stomach, time to think about what was going to happen to him and Pete and Harris and all the others.

Time squeezed and lengthened, perfectly elastic – one minute could stretch into eternity while the next passed in a blur.

As if by mutual consent the talking stopped. Harris passed out small tots of rum and the men took it in any container they could find. Bryan accepted his measure in a battered soup can and then passed it to Pete, encouraging the chalk-faced boy to take a draught of the drink.

Bryan watched as Harris checked his watch and brought a

whistle to his lips. He stood on the bottom rung of the ladder holding his revolver, one foot on the step.

The bombing stopped.

Silence.

Peace.

The sounds of summer filtered through; birdsong and the rustle of wind through grass.

The whole world rocked with an explosion that pushed a cloud of dust over the trenches, passed over their heads like an angel of death. Some of the men cheered, but not many. Most of them stood in silence, still licking the last drop of rum from their lips. Then the whistles began to blow.

Up and down the line – whistles. Harris was already halfway up the ladder, shouting, screaming at them: "Come on, come on now."

He stuck his head over the parapet, still looking back down to his men. They all heard the heavy thud and saw his helmet fall. Harris's head sheared away, a geyser of warm blood splashed down on their upturned faces.

Pete screamed then threw up his rum.

Already someone had Harris's pistol; Richard Jims, waving the revolver above his head like a trophy – shouting at them to get up there as he pulled himself up two rungs at a time.

"See," he shouted. He stood on top of the trench, toes peering over the edge as he towered above them. "See," he screamed and then turned around to face the Hun. In a second he had passed from sight.

Bryan picked up the mud-caked rifle that was propped up beside him. He waited patiently at the bottom of the ladder for his turn, an orderly queue. He pushed Pete in front of him, his hand in the centre of the kid's back because however horrible it was out there, it would be worse to be taken back by one of the Redcaps, escorted through the communications trench where the court martial would be brief.

At the top of the ladder the wind pulled at Bryan, threatening to push him back down, his frail, fatigue-torn body offering little resistance. Gun smoke hung in the air like an early morning mist, hiding whatever was ahead of him.

Bryan stood on the brow of the trench for a moment, trying to calm himself. Men pushed past him, eager to get to the front, to find the glory that awaited them amongst the mud and pools of stagnant water.

Bryan walked forward, caught up in the lines of men who marched straight ahead. There was no talking, no jokes. This was what they trained for. In front of him rows of men marched with their rifles held to arms.

The sound of a machine gun split the air, lazily turned over in the summer warmth.

He heard the heavy thud as bullets smacked into the front rows, the cries of the men calling as much in surprise as pain. Ahead of him the solid line of men broke – one rake of the machine gun and the first row of men fell. It returned for a second pass, like a scythe cutting through the lines, leaving one or two men, who still marched forwards.

Bryan continued – to his right marched Pete, matching his step, staring straight ahead, as if he could see what was going to happen to him but didn't understand it. The boy clung to his rifle, wrapped his arms around it and stomped on. Bryan checked across to his left – most of his line held.

He stumbled on something and the fall dragged him to his knees. Jims lay on the ground, bleeding from his arm and neck and everywhere the bullets had burrowed into him. He was already dead, his face frozen in a shocked stare as if certain of his immortality until the very moment of his death.

Men walked past Jims on either side, a rush of bodies marching forward. Bryan gave the dead man one last look and then rose to join his companions.

The lines were not so straight now – a confused muddle of men walked to their own internal parade drum. Of the twenty who had started out with him from the trenches, five had already fallen. Bryan heard the machine gun return to its path and men on his left and right dropped to the ground screaming.

Pete fell. Bryan watched as the boy struggled to staunch the flow of blood from a hole in his side. They had orders – don't attend to the casualties, keep on and take the objective, the medics would be sent out after each wave to clear the battlefield of the injured. Leave it to them.

Harris's orders.

Bryan dropped his rifle down beside the body of the boy.

"It hurts," Pete said. His tunic was already black with blood, such a small hole, just a puncture. His face was drained of colour and when he looked up he seemed unable to focus.

Bryan took out a vial of iodine, soaked a length of bandage in the brown fluid and then pressed it into the boy's wound. Pete screamed in pain and maybe it was already too late.

"You've got to go on," Pete said. No stirring words, no reason.

Bryan pressed Pete's hands down hard on the wound; blood bubbled up around the boy's fingers.

"You've got to go on," Pete said. His voice was softer now – hardly a whisper above the guns and the shells and the screaming.

Bryan stood up, picked up his rifle and continued his march without looking back at Pete.

The sound of the machine gun was louder now, nearer, and Bryan walked forward expecting with each step to feel the thud of a bullet in his chest. The gun had shattered the once military straight lines. Men stumbled forward. To Bryan's right a man cried out and fell to the ground clutching the air with his fists as if to capture the breaths that escaped from his lungs.

At last, discipline broke down. The mad, endless trudge forwards was over and in hysteria the men began to run; shouting, firing rifles wildly, screaming and then finally dying.

Bryan ran forward with the others, frightened of being left behind. Running, running toward the gunfire and the enemy, his rifle hanging limp and useless from his shoulder, bumping against his hips as he dodged craters and bodies, losing his balance, lurching forward, and then regaining his footing. On and on. Tears streaming down his face. Expecting to hit barbed wire or trenches, or to feel the searing violation of a bullet as it tore into him.

Nothing.

On and on, over the battle-scarred earth.

Bryan tripped on the pitted ground but there was nothing to stop his charge through the gun smoke, never seeing more than a few yards ahead of him.

On and on, until the clouds broke to reveal only untouched ground and the summer sun.

It was quiet: the stammer of the machine gun and the screaming of dying men had ceased. Instead, there were only the sounds of peace. Overhead a bird cawed, a small animal disturbed the hedgerow.

He walked through a field where the green shoots of the crop were just beginning to show through the dark brown soil. Beyond that were a short wooden fence and a clump of trees with their yellow shoots budding on green branches. And beyond that was the graveyard. He walked forward, slowly.

Ahead of him were simple white crosses, too numerous to count. A crop of markers in lines like those the men once formed on the parade ground.

He walked along the paths that crossed the site, reading the names to himself.   Pte Matthew Stanwell, 1/7/16; Pte Stephen Hanratty, 1/7/16.

He walked down the next aisle, for every name he knew there were a hundred unfamiliar to him, their lives a mystery. But the others...

Pte Peter Franklin, 1/7/16; Cpl Ian Harris, 1/7/16; Pte Richard Jims, 1/7/16; Pte Bryan Lamb, 1/7/16.

His own cross, just like the others; pure white.

The cross shone like bleached bones. Bryan knelt down in front of the grave, *his grave*, the French sun quickly drying his uniform.

Bryan searched through his pocket and found the letter to Kathleen, folded in on itself for protection.

He left the letter by Pete's cross, and beside it the mud-encrusted rifle. Neither of them would be of any further use to him.

Bryan retraced his steps, through the copse and over the fence and into a field, where mist hung low over a carpet of unkempt grass. He could hear the sounds of battle once more, the cries of pain and the snap of gunfire. He could smell the battle, the stink of cordite and blood, growing stronger as he walked into the mist.

The Wake Up Call
Alison J. Hill

He wasn't thinking straight really, it was all too much.

This sort of thing doesn't happen to people like me, he thought to himself as he slowly unscrewed the top off the petrol can. His hands were shaking, sweating too, making it difficult to unfasten the canister.

"For God's sake... open... Christ almighty!" he shouted to himself.

He stopped momentarily, looking round to see if anyone was nearby. No, he was pretty sure no one would be around these parts at this time of morning, and especially not in this awful weather... no, he was the only one stupid enough to be out at this time; he was banking on the chance that it would all go unnoticed. Well at least until the deed was done. *God, a stiff drink would go down well just now*, he thought to himself.

He stepped away from his car, wondering if he'd poured enough petrol over it to conceal the evidence. He made a mental note 'remember to always carry more than one canister around in the future.'

God, what am I thinking? I'm not about to let this happen again. But it's not my fault; I wouldn't be here now if it wasn't for that stupid...

He gathered himself, and took a last look around before sticking his head through the window of his car. He then ignited his lighter, his exact throw saw the lighter land on the dash board, and immediately the dash burst into flames.

He was surprised as to how quickly the flames took a hold, a cue therefore to get the hell out of there.

He ran off through the woods and into the open fields, which he knew would eventually lead down to the main road. He felt sick and stopped to throw up; looking back over his shoulder he could see a cloud of black smoke billowing high above the tree line. He wiped his mouth with the back of his hand and continued to make his way towards the road. He could hear sirens. *God, surely not already, that would be too quick.* His heart sank, as he suddenly realised the sirens were likely to be for her...

Eventually he arrived at the main road; he could stop running now, but he needed to appear rational, not draw attention to himself. He pulled his coat collar up around his neck and stuck his hands in his pockets; home was a good two miles from here which would take him about half an hour at reasonable pace. He was thankful he didn't have to go up the Old Port Road, walking past there just at the moment wasn't what he needed.

But what do I need? What could possibly make me feel better, apart from an opportunity to turn back the hands of time? he thought to himself.

The answer? Nothing... nothing was going to change what he'd done. He was thinking hard now, maybe it would have been better to have just called an ambulance, but then that would have had disastrous consequences, those extra few drinks would not have gone unnoticed on the breathalyser.

It was better this way, no one would know it was him, how could they possibly?

His mind drifted to thoughts of the woman... *Have I killed her? If I have, was it outright or did she suffer first? Or maybe... I haven't killed her, maybe she'll be alright... but if she's OK, will that mean she'll be able to identify me? Oh God I feel sick again...*

He stopped in his tracks and tried to gather himself; after a few deep breaths he managed to take his mind off throwing up again.

The walk home felt like hours instead of minutes. Finally, as he neared his house, he spotted his neighbour approaching with her dog.

Shit, how am I going to explain this? he thought. She was a typical nosy neighbour, never missed a trick, and she knew what time he left for work in a morning.

She's bound to want to know what I'm doing walking back home, he thought. *I wonder if she's noticed that my car has gone? Maybe I could say that I'm not well and that I've nipped to the shop for some paracetamol. But if she saw me leave in the car, she'll be wondering where it is? Oh God, what am I going to do?... wait, just wait and see what she says first...*

The woman smiled as she approached him. "Morning, Roy, what are you up to? I thought you'd left for work already."

"Erm... morning, Mrs. Lambert. I... yes... I did leave early this morning, but well I... had to take my car in for repair and I've just got the bus back home. I've got the day off, and lots to do so... I'd better get back and get cracking."

Mrs Lambert laughed. "OK, well enjoy your day off, perhaps you could–"

Roy didn't give her chance to finish her sentence. As he began to walk away, she called back to him, "Perhaps you could pop in for a cup of coffee later if you're off all day?"

"Thank you, Mrs. Lambert, but I plan on being very busy today," Roy shouted back without bothering to turn round.

Thank God she didn't ask too many questions, he thought to himself. *Now the next hurdle is to phone the police, and hope they don't ask too many questions either.*

Roy opened his front door, his dog rushed up to meet him, sporting a look of confusion at his master's early return, but also wagging his tail in anticipation of an extra walk. Roy walked straight past the animal, his mind focused on what he needed to do.

Trouble was, he just couldn't think straight, his mind wasn't actually focused at all.

He made his way into the kitchen, turned on the tap, and quickly gulped down a glass of water, but that wasn't enough to calm him, he needed more. Thinking quickly, he rushed over to the other side of the kitchen, pulled open the door and grabbed a whiskey bottle. He unscrewed the top and took a few long swigs. As the liquor hit the back of his throat it felt comforting, a familiar warm sensation travelled down his gullet, and for a few seconds, it made him feel nonchalant. He continued to guzzle away, trusting that this feeling of carelessness would make everything alright again. But a few seconds was all it would be, before he knew it, he was vomiting again, all down his clothes.

He ran back to the sink and splashed cold water over his face, it felt soothing, and he tried again to collect his thoughts. He still had to report the car as stolen, but he just wasn't ready to make the call. He decided to take a shower and change his clothes first; they carried a putrid stench, a combination of petrol and vomit. He took them off where he stood and shoved everything into the washing machine.

Standing under the shower provided solace; the jets of hot water hit his body leaving him feeling revived and alert but also privy to the cruel provocation of what he'd done.

He wanted to stay in there forever, anything would be better than having to deal with the cold truth. He walked into his bedroom and closed the curtains, it was like shutting the world out and it felt good. He lay down on his bed and shut his eyes. He searched his mind trying desperately to make sense of it all.

Despite everything, he found sleep, albeit unsettled, but fifteen minutes later he woke abruptly... to the sound of knocking. Someone else was in his house, he was certain.

He strained to listen but the silence was almost deafening, he could hear the dog growling and the sound of his stairs creaking. His stomach turned.

Christ someone is coming up the stairs, he thought. He tried to move but something stopped him, he hadn't a clue what, and his efforts to fight it were futile. The footsteps reached his bedroom door, and he could feel his heart pounding against his chest. The door opened...

It was her, the woman from the accident. He could see her face plainly as the daylight from the landing briefly lit up his room.

Her face was streaked with blood and he could make out cuts and abrasions through her mangled clothes. She was shouting at him, but he couldn't hear what she was saying. He could see tears spilling out onto her cheeks. He wanted to calm her, and he tried to talk softly to her, but she couldn't seem to hear him either, then suddenly... she lunged forward grabbing him around his throat. He clutched at her arms, trying frantically to release her grip, but it was no good, she was too powerful and he began to feel himself losing consciousness as a sense of appeasement induced.

The surreality bated as amidst the horror he could hear his telephone ringing. It seemed to get louder and louder until suddenly he realised... he was dreaming.

He sat bolt upright, he was breathing heavily, and sweat poured down his face stinging his eyes. He took a moment to rally himself and then picked up the phone.

"Hello?"

"Roy, its Michael are you OK?"

"Michael... Michael, who?"

"Michael, your boss who, why aren't you at work?"

"Oh God, sorry Michael, I was sleeping, I've not been well over night, I was going to ring but..."

"Look, don't worry mate, I thought you must be ill, but I just wanted to make sure you were OK. Just take a few days and I'll see you when you're better."

"OK, Michael... cheers... see you in a couple of days."

Roy wiped the sweat from his forehead and made his way to the bathroom. He held a flannel under the cold tap, wrung it out, and placed it across his forehead. He stared at himself in his shaving mirror. The dream had sure terrified him and he still had to make the phone call.

He wandered back into his bedroom, picked up the phone, and dialled the number for the local police station. His hands were shaking and his mouth parched. The person on the other end of the line spoke, and Roy wanted desperately to hang up, but something urged him to proceed and report his car stolen.

"So let me get this straight, Mr. Harpur, you looked out of your window this morning to find your car had been stolen?"

"Yes, that's correct."

"OK, I'll take all the details and if we hear anything someone will be in touch."

Roy felt slightly better for finally making the call; he sighed deeply, and sat down on the edge of his bed. All he could do now was wait for someone to report his burnt out car to the police, and... bingo... job done, he could go on with his life as though nothing had ever happened. All this would eventually fade in his memory, and he would just have to learn to live with it that's all.

Just then his phone rang again. Roy's stomach turned over, *could this be the police already?*

He just couldn't bring himself to pick the receiver up.

I'll let the answer phone get it, then I'll play it back later, he thought to himself.

He made his way down stairs and put the kettle on, doing his best to carry on as normal; his dog followed him around the kitchen, still hopeful for another walk.

After he finished his tea, he picked up the phone. If the police had called, he really needed to know what they'd said, and he was desperate for some sort of closure.

Sure enough someone had left a message; he pressed the button and listened...

"Hi, Roy, it's Andy from Barton's Garage. Just to let you know your car is ready, but to save you another bus trip, Jill our new receptionist is going to drop it back to you. She only lives on the Old Port Road, so she can walk it home from yours. So anyway, if you're not in, I'll get her to push the keys through the letter box. Cheers then mate, bye."

Roy couldn't believe his ears. *How could it be? How could his car possibly be at the garage after he set it alight and watched it burst into flames?* He listened again, just to make sure he was hearing correctly.

Just then there was a knock at the door. He made his way through the hall to the front door. As he approached, he could see the silhouette of a woman standing at the door. *This must be the receptionist*; part of him wanted to wait until she'd gone, but his curiosity got the better of him.

He opened the door and there standing on his door step was the woman from his dream, the woman he thought he'd knocked down earlier that morning. Roy stood there, shocked.

"Hi, I think Andy from the garage phoned and left you a message."

Roy couldn't answer, he was totally speechless.

"I'm Jill, I've come to drop your car back." She handed Roy an envelope. "He said there were a couple of advisements, but it's passed OK. Oh and the invoice is in there too."

Roy still didn't know what to say. He looked over at his car; sure enough it was certainly his. He looked back at Jill trying to make sense of it all.

"Are you okay, Mr Harpur? You look like you've seen a ghost."

Finally Roy spoke, "Oh... yes, sorry love, I was miles away. Thank you... thank you very much."

He watched the woman walk off up the avenue and then went over to his car. There wasn't a mark on it, not a burn, scratch... nothing.

How can it possibly be? he thought to himself. *It's absurd, completely absurd.*

He quickly went back inside his house, poured a glass of whiskey, and sat down.

Could the whole thing have been a dream? Did I knock her

down? Did I torch my car? Maybe it was a premonition, no... a warning?

At that point he realised that the whole thing was a figment of his own paranoia. He looked at the whiskey glass. "No more of this stuff for me," he said to himself.

As he poured away what was left in the glass and the bottle down the sink, he suddenly had an awful thought... *The police, oh God, the police. How am I going to explain that one?*

He plucked up the courage to phone the police, and concocted a story; he told them that his friend had taken the car and he'd forgotten all about it. Of course he apologised profusely and accepted a ticking off from a very nice WPC on the other end of the phone. Something about wasting police time and making more of an effort to keep track of his car in the future, but he wasn't bothered, he was just glad that it had all been in his mind.

Later on that afternoon, after mulling things over, he realised that his excessive drinking had gotten so out of control that he'd become paranoid and didn't like that, not one bit. It was the biggest wake up call he could possibly have.

He picked up the phone directory and flicked through it, then picked up his phone and dialled a number.

After a few rings the person on the other end answered.

"Good afternoon, Alcoholics Anonymous, how may I help you?"

The Gallery
Conrad Williams

It was the third week in a row that I had put Marley off. I could tell she wasn't happy about it; she had asked me to come with her to the Bead with a resigned sigh, expecting the answer I dutifully supplied. As a sweetener, I threw her a line about meeting up later without knowing whether I would or not. It clinched the requisite smile, anyway.

"Okay," she said, coming over to straighten my collar and press the back of her hand against the polymer cast of my half-mask. I could almost imagine the chill of her flesh. "Meet me at four thirty, by the Bead entrance. We'll get Shopped for half an hour."

"Great," I said heavily, but not without a smile.

"What are you going to do with your day?" she asked, an ironic slant to her eyebrows, "as if I didn't know?"

"I'm going to the Gallery," I said, maybe a bit too defensively, "and then I thought I might go to Rouffe's place for a few hours."

Her smile disappeared. "Rouffe? Jesus, Cloake, I thought you'd given that up. Can't you just be satisfied with the Gallery? Why do you have to filthy yourself up with Oldstuff?" She almost choked on the word but she managed to steer herself back on course. "You know what'll happen to you if the– "

"Yes," I said, gently propelling her towards the Chute. "I know what will happen to me if the Hoods find out. Look at me, I'm trembling like the last leaf on the tree."

"I'll not watch you die," she said. "I'm getting tired of you taking all these risks." And her parting shot, as she was vacced out of sight into the Chute, wrapped in her shiny green cagoule like a clot of snot hawked up a nostril: "You're a fool, Cloake! A bastard fool!"

And maybe I am. We get a bad press, us fools. But what's so

harmful about being a simple soul who wants to keep a grip of yesterday? I like sunsets, when I can get up on the roof to see over the cluttered mess of the city to see one. I like rain, although not this discoloured, stinging stuff that spoils the window frames and makes the air smell of brimstone. I don't like change. I don't really like the Gallery but that's as close as we're allowed to get to our past. Which is why I like Rouffe.

After Marley had gone, I had a second cup of coffee and shaved in front of the mirror, gingerly peeling back the lower edges of my mask to get at the tricky hairs there where my skin wasn't too mangled. I gently lubed the rubber seal that houses my bad eye, which isn't really an eye at all, but a tiny camera whose fibres have been Organifused with the few optical nerves I have left. A fair job, but I have a problem with colours out of that side. Not that there are any colours left in the city worth looking at.

I pulled on a jumper and a woollen beanie, stuffed a deck of credits in my pocket without bothering to count them and had a quick look around the flat to see if I'd forgotten anything. The pristine walls, the dehumanised, ultra-hygienic whiff of nothing at all made me feel ill. For the nth time I dreaded returning and sleeping under the heated airduvet, the warm breath in my lungs being replaced by recycled, refrigerated alien stuff pumped out of the bowels of the city. I could resist, if I wanted to; strike out on my own. I never had to see this cubicle again. But for Marley...

I fed myself into the Chute thinking of vacuum packaging and sterilisation techniques and waxen, mirthless faces telling me how great it was to be alive, have another course of injections why don't you?

I flew Wasps during Petal Dawn. You heard right. Petal Dawn. Don't ask me who was fighting... Cowboys v Indians, Cops v Robbers, Us v Them. Same as always. Does it matter?

We were a cure. We were the magic dust that turns water into wine. One day, a Metropolis stood by a river's edge. It might have been called London; I don't remember. By the following morning we'd razed it. Fires cleansed one thousand square miles of rat-infested alleys of crime. I don't even know why we did it. We were conscripted. Those who could fly were given things to fly. We were shown targets and told to sting them. We stung them. We got medals. If we refused, we were shaken by the hand and fed along a conveyor belt into a wet, red, watertight room where they kept the rotating blades. I had no choice.

Wow, they used to say regardless, *brave chap, jolly well done.* Until I drop this on them: I shot down the ArcticAir behemoth, flight 349. When they hear that, it's like they've just been fed a teaspoon of dog's vomit, the way their smiles dissolve.

After 349, I spent a long time giving the neck of a bottle serious love bites, pumped my veins full of memory-blocking colours and shapes. At some point, hobbling in the scavenging dark of my conscience and the cratered no-man's land beyond the city parameters, I'd thrown myself in front of a freight train. I'd been out of it so long, I hadn't even *noticed* the new city being built around me until I woke up in one of its hospitals, looking like some kind of human anemone, there were so many tubes sticking out of and into me.

"Look, Marley," I said, drugged up to my one good eyeball, "this tube is the important one. See? It's important because..." I leaned towards her, lots of theatre, and whispered, "... because... *it doesn't go anywhere.*"

Marley had found me. She'd picked me up, picked up the shattered shell of my face and carried me on her back, a mile, to the casualty bays where my head was slotted back together. I still wasn't sure who she was.

"Hush," Marley whispered to me on the first insufferable nights away from any of my crutches. "It's all right now. You can start to forget. Try not to suffer."

I tried not to suffer. Gradually, I rallied. I began to forget. I began to escape from the suffering.

Yeah. Really.

Something I never told anyone. Maybe so there'd be no compassion, maybe so I'd suffer rightly for my unforgivable sin. My parents were on that flight.

I walked backstreets. The concrete is orange-blue here, wet with rain and a collision of light from the Zeps floating above the city and the neon slabs that cluster beneath most of the roofs. I don't like the main drags. The traffic is noisy, dirty and dangerous. Like the people.

The Gallery is on DWay>. It's a little far to walk, but I don't mind. There are extra risks. Anywhere that isn't < (*central* to sign-haters such as myself) is apt to be patrolled heavily by Hoods. They don't like to see you loning it; prefer it if you were shepherded around in a terrorist-targeted bus. I've been stopped occasionally. On one memorable evening, I was strip-searched on AWay>, which is as close as you can get to the inner roads without actually being on them. They were suspicious about the mask. Thought it was a disguise. I've got to know some of the Hoods quite well. Some of them have the courtesy to flash you a badge before crowning you with their voltcoshes.

I slipped out of CWay> and hurried past a cluster of kids on the corner of the street. While they were busy pelting a dog with stones, they might not pay much attention to me. The Gallery made itself known via a flat disc of cool metal slotted into the wall outside its window. When you touched it with your special subscriber's key, it made a faint gong-like echo and deducted 500 credits from your bank account — or in my case, Marley's bank account. The entire partition of glass slid down into a housing and let me through, wincing, as I always did, when I imagined the glass malfunctioning and shooting back up to cleave me in two.

Halve was at the desk, a sloping bank of white underlit on her side which made her face seem longer. She was wearing a grape-coloured chenille jumper and soft, anthracite slacks that made me want to reach out and stroke her.

"Catalogue?" she asked, pushing a wedge of thick brown hair

behind her ear. She wasn't fazed by the mask. Most people weren't. There were a lot of them around. I could never get used to them getting so used to me.

I nodded and she handed me a foolscap glossy white plastic folder with an off-white matte lower case 'g' embossed in the bottom right hand corner. Inside was a single page, stitched into the spine with purple thread. I stroked the paper. Smelled it, not caring what Halve thought. It smelled new, antiseptic. It read:

20th century Miserablists

or

The Hard-boiled 'Tec

"Are you getting anything else in?" I asked Halve.

"We've got the carb analysis lab working on some new fragments. Some kind of romantic text, they believe. And some tosh they found deep underground in a steel drum. Hardbacks by a dud called Archer. There was a sign on it, barely readable, but they reckon it said 'PRICE SLASHED'." She laughed. I did too. Just to give my mouth something to do; I didn't know what she was talking about.

"I'll go with the Miserablist stuff," I said, "just to counter the non-stop comedy of my life."

She gave me a look then slid an obsidian key into a socket. There was a lovely, snug 'thunk' sound and I felt a hum surge through my feet.

"Gallery One," she said.

I gave the catalogue back to Halve and padded past a few security apes who nodded at me without looking me in the eye. An archway gave on to an expansive room floored with lacquered parquet. Heated air wafted at me, urged on by giant fans clinging to the roof, fifty feet above the ground. I headed for the bank of screens at the top end. As I neared, the power surge reached a peak and they stuttered into life, seeds of blue light scattering across a liquid black background. A montage of letters evolved out of the gloop of light: a story title and an author. *The Mainstream*, it was called, by some Pen called Nicholas Royle. I read for a while, my fingers itching to hold paper, my nostrils thwarted by the lack of input. When my eye reached the bottom of the screen, the words dissolved and were replaced by more. The story hissed and stuttered its meaning into me. It was a frustrating, yet edifying experience. I followed the complex peaks and troughs of the story like a pilot absorbs pitch and roll and yaw.

Feeling that my actions were being governed by some other person exterior to me, I turned and got back into the car.

I nodded at the words without fully understanding, trusting the narrator with the same helpless love a dog bestows upon its owner. That was part of the buzz for me, clinging to the peccadilloes of a language that was dying, or already dead.

There was another story, called *Common Land*, by a Pen called Joel Lane, another, *More Tomorrow*, by Michael Marshall Smith. I wondered if Rouffe had his fingers into any of this. The authors' pictures, rendered in washy pixels, came into view, floating out of the Boolean soup like weak discs of fat floating on the surface of one of Rouffe's casseroles. Faces of writers dead a century or so. God, why did they look so wasted, so starved?

I sensed someone else in the room with me, and glanced right. A woman nestled into a deep fleece, her blonde hair and a moist slice of lip discernible at the curve of her hood, was mouthing the words spread across her screen. She glanced at me, smiled, returned to her screen. I went over to her and said hello. She was reading a story by some Pen called Williams.

"Look at this," she said, gesturing at a passage that swam on the screen's purplish surface.

"Christ," I breathed, impressed. "Miserable *bastard*."

"Isn't he?" she said. "You should read his later stuff. You'd slash your wrists." She read on a little more and then: "Miserable, *miserable* bastard."

I liked her. We talked some more and I eyed her up best I could, even though she was on my wrong side. She had a scar on the bridge of her nose. Her eyes were dark blue, the colour of storm water. She had big, meaty lips, bow-shaped. Nice.

"I'm Cloake," I said and shook her hand.

"Keri."

"I haven't seen you around before," I said.

"Well, that beats 'Do you come here often?'" She nodded, looking me up and down, appraising me. Did I like that? Mmm, just a little bit. Keri shrugged her head out of the hood; a lot of hair – more than I'd anticipated – followed it. She looked around her. "You haven't seen me because I generally come here late at night, well after the place has closed down. I have a pass."

"Whoa," I said. "Privileged woman."

"That's right. My father owns this place, and a few others out in the Belt. You should see them."

"Not much chance of that is there? Hoods here are very protective of the chicks in their nest. Like, they don't want anybody leaving it."

"There are ways."

I nodded. "Like I said... 'privileged woman'."

"I could take you one day, if you're interested." She raised her eyebrows. I caught a whiff of something – peaches.

"I don't know. I'm quite happy with this place."

"You should try broadening your horizons."

I thought of Rouffe. "I do okay."

After a while, our verbal tennis match coming along beautifully, one of the security apes came and stood next to me. "Time's up, Joe," he monotoned.

"But I haven't finished."

"So read more quickly."

I didn't argue. It was a routine we had. Keri wasn't going to stick around too long either; I heard her footsteps creaking on the floorboards as I tipped a wink at Halve and made my way outside.

"So I can't tempt you?" Keri called, replacing her hood and drifting backwards away from me: she was heading for the nest of alleyways that would lead her towards H, J or KWay. All right for some.

"I'll be here tomorrow. Same time, if you want to tell me more. I'll buy you a coffee. Or whatever passes for it these days."

"Deal," she said. She turned and strode away, raising a hand after a while. I liked that too. That she had the confidence, or temerity, to know I'd still be watching her. I liked a lot about her.

Time to share a secret. The only reason I go to the Gallery is to take some heat off me. I reckon that if I'm seen by the Hoods in a controlled literary haven, I'll be able to give them the slip when I hit a hardcore joint such as Rouffe's. *Such as*. Now there's a laugh. I don't know of anyone else dealing in Oldstuff. Don't know that many people around who have a clue as to what Oldstuff is. Why I have any interest in it is all wrapped up in my parents. Call it sentimental claptrap, call it a sad old bastard running to seed looking for a way to punish himself for what he did. Call it atonement. My father was a novelist. Not a great one, but he was able to spin a yarn good as the next Pen. He could get people turning pages, which is what counts I suppose, so it doesn't matter one jot to me that he didn't win any literary prizes or shining critical notices. Each book he put out had an audience of sorts and as long as he had a manuscript to deliver, his publishers were always happy to keep his contracts topped up, even though he was never going to be on their A-list. Maybe another reason for going to the Gallery was to one day punch up a story of my father's, one of the last real Pens before the Hoods drew a line under the final chapter and closed the book. It's for exactly the same reason, and perhaps one or two more, that I haunt Rouffe's grotto.

Getting to Rouffe's is not easy. In fact, it is a grade-A bitch. If there are Hoods around, you have to forget it. The merest threat of heat in Rouffe's patch could wind up with his grotto in dust, him executed and yours truly in clink for the rest of my natural. But trust me, the risks are worth it.

There's a railway runs through the city, long disused but still accessible. I slipped off DWay< and, checking all the while for Zeps and Hoods, I slid and swore my way down the embankment, as conspicuous as a smear of shit on wedding cake. At the bottom, afforded token concealment by a denuded rhododendron bush and straggled ranks of bastard cabbage, I scanned the sky once more then struck out along the rails, which stretched to a sharp point in the distance on either side of sleepers coated in a thin fall of snow from the previous night. I had to pick my way round hillocks of litter and junk, in varying stages of decay. There were a few bodies down here; I tried my best to ignore the frozen outstretched limbs that jutted from the undergrowth like motifs of supplication on a church hoarding. At one point I came across a Cessna, concertinaed into the embankment. The pilot's body was still in the cockpit, hands gripping the steering column; his head was a scarlet bloom on the fuselage prow, like a religious icon decorated from behind by the crushed radials of the propeller.

It was getting on, the sun a pale suggestion behind the bank of insistent cloud. A sequence of grey blocks marked the south section of the city, rising into the sky like a vertical pavement. I wouldn't have much time before I had to meet Marley back at the Bead; missing her would not be a good idea. A fragile type, Marley would find reasons, true or otherwise, to attack the tissues that bonded us, perhaps exposing deep-seated facts about ourselves that neither of us were equipped to cope with. Not yet anyway. We were both – thanks to different phantoms – deeply unstable people, picking our way through the ruins of the city, trying to absorb something real and solid to act as a foundation upon which we might rebuild our shattered lives. That I could be so rational and accepting of my inconsistencies was my advantage; that Marley could recognise her lapses into melancholy was hers.

I surfaced, ever so slowly, at XWay>, at the edge of a maze of estates and factories which ringed the hub of the southern section of the city. There was hardly anyone around. I jinked down a few side streets, looped back on myself, stood on the bridge over the canal and watched the rainbows stream beneath me. I sat in Concrete Park and looked at the concrete birds and the concrete cars and the concrete people.

I waited. It didn't take long this time. I stared into the bank of fences and walls, their shape and substance lost to a miasma of colour, courtesy of the local graffiti artists, or so Rouffe liked the Hoods to think. Pretty soon, trying to force the limits of my focus beyond the solid bank of patterns ahead, Rouffe's grotto was made known to me. He was using the same access as last week which was possibly a risk but more possibly the work of a man with more nerve than me. The door shimmered out of the swirl of paints, assuming a clarity that had, moments ago, been a blur. The illusion beaten, I could return my eyes to their relaxed state and still see the door – and, as always, wonder how I could possibly have missed it or how anyone could walk by without clocking it.

My fingers itched; I smelled ghosts, but I managed to still my enthusiasm in favour of one final look round. Satisfied that I was alone, I drifted over to the door and tapped it with my fingernail three times... two times... three times.

"Open Sesame," I murmured, as Rouffe worked his magic and the colours absorbed me.

I'll not give you a thumbnail regarding Rouffe. Form your own opinion. From the way he speaks, construct his build, his looks, the way he dresses. Describing my friend would seem too much like providing the authorities with an IdentFrame to plot his capture. All you need to know about Rouffe is that he loves literature and he loves it real. He scoffs when I tell him I've been to the Gallery. Rightly so. Because once he's stopped ridiculing my virtual relationships, he takes me to his basement and shows me a pile of carpet tiles. As always, he'll pull a few away to reveal a tea chest.

In the tea chest are carefully wrapped books. Real books. Out of their housings of cellophane and brown paper, sitting in the cup of my hands (their immanent weight so comfortable you'd think my flesh were designed for such moments) I can smell the suggestion of real worlds, far beyond the pared down, pale and petrified coma world I pass through today with all the commitment and vigour of a man at an MWay service station. I turn the pages, Rouffe chuckling at my patent aggrandisement, and in each ring of tea or coffee, each pencilled comment in the margin, each pressed flower I can cling to what is human in me. This, more than any amount of current social interaction helps me to shape the way I must live my future. No, strike that, it just helps me to live. God knows how far I would have gone to snuffing myself out before Marley, before Rouffe.

"I can't stay long," I said.

"You never do," Rouffe replied, sitting in front of the battered bank of hard drives and monitors that helped maintain the shield he hid behind. "And I'd rather you didn't. Two people talking is more noise than I'm happy with."

I took one of the books over to an armchair and read for twenty minutes although I couldn't relax enough to digest most of what it was trying to relate. It didn't matter; the simple textures of paper and ink and dust jacket subsumed by my fingertips seemed much richer than any of the book's codes or narratives or styles.

I took some tea with Rouffe and we chatted about the Hoods and how restrictions and laws in the city were becoming so tight, soon my visits would have to stop because they would no longer be any pedestrian activity. I realised my fingers were straying to the spines of the books, massaging them as if trying to make supple again what the centuries had made brittle. Rouffe's voice was a burble of thick consonants and fluting vowels, its rhythm a counterpoint to all the angles and discords in my life. When the clock chimed four, even the haste with which I jumped from my seat seemed Morphean, unreal.

"I must go. Marley... she'll be livid if I don't keep our

appointment."

Rouffe simply nodded and simpered, the inherent message being that he would see me again.

"You'll be here?" I asked, but I didn't linger to find out. I pulled on my jacket and slipped outside, waiting for the colours in the wall to spit me clear. Rouffe would be there. He always was.

The Bead made itself known to me as I turned the corner into UWay<, a building with a huge dome runnelled with black lines: a huge egg wrapped in a web. The lines were Vac Chutes, designed with punctuative chambers that delivered you to the shop of your choice. By the time I made it to the entrance – a gilded arc festooned with carved flowers and cherubs, further decorated with fountains that sprayed coloured water – I was ten minutes late. Marley was standing by the mouth of the Vac Chute, arguing with a Hood who, presumably, had become irritated by her lack of purpose.

"It's okay!" I called, jogging over and trying to smile. "She's no vagrant. No terrorist. She's with me. We're going to get Shopped. It's fine, really." The Hood gave me a once over with those awful, nictitating eyes and then asked to see our papers with a voice that was raspily metallic. The quilted wrap that guarded his nose and mouth was grey and ragged. Something squirmed out of a fold and squirmed straight back in again. I handed over our ID discs, trying my best not to touch the bastard.

Reluctantly, he nodded us through and I thanked him profusely. I'd heard the rumours of internal body searches and interrogations so brutal they'd left the victims psychologically scarred. I didn't want any of that; I propelled Marley through the entrance and sealed her in the chute, programming the capsules to travel in tandem. As the journey began, Marley's chastisement of my lateness scalding my ears, I thought I saw Keri drifting across the plaza. Concealed by her voluminous coat, she was being followed by two Hoods. She wouldn't hear if I shouted a warning but then we were scooped up over the top of the building and all I could see was sky and the silver glint of credit decks as they waited to swallow our money.

We arrived back at the dorm as night spilled its guts across the city. Marley was in no mood for soft talk or getting naked and I couldn't blame her. I'd been a shit. On top of the Hood incident, I'd been distracted during the entire Bead trip, showing little interest in her purchases or the whole rigmarole of the 'sale suits' making their pitches at us from podia dotted around the various showrooms.

She went for a shower and I sat by the Com, wishing I'd asked Keri for her number. I contacted the Gallery and talked to Halve but she wasn't allowed to divulge customer information.

"But I'm worried," I protested, "I think she might be in trouble."

"With the Hoods? Then she ought to be more prudent where her misdemeanours are concerned." Halve's voice was as glossy and featureless as the catalogues she managed. There was no point trying to convince her of the corruptibility of the Hoods and their network; I downed the link and sent a signal to Rouffe's node.

"Forget her," he said, when I told him what I'd seen, "she means nothing to you and if she's being tracked by Hoods then you don't need that kind of excitement in your life. Not that I give a fig for your well-being, you understand. But a link to you is a link to me and, my friend, I'm not quite ready to be put in a state where a machine is doing my breathing for me. So desist. Forthwith. Keep your grubby little fingers where Marley can see them."

The link downed, I lay back on the floor and listened to the water jets playing in the bathroom. Tomorrow I would have to go back to the Gallery and see if she turned up there. If she didn't, I would have to work on Halve, coax some information out of her.

"Who was that on the Com, darling?" Marley said, emerging from a bank of steam. I could tell she was pissed off. She only ever called me 'darling' when she was narked about something.

"Rouffe," I said. "Check the datatape for yourself if you don't believe me."

"Ooh, defensive mode. Something to hide."

It would be easier to handle if that last shot had come over as a question. Instead, I shrugged myself deeper into the newsbites on the VDU. Over it all I could only think of Keri. And feel bad about my unspoken obligation to Marley. I'd betrayed her though nothing had happened. But maybe I needed this dilemma to prove how I truly felt for the woman who had saved my life. For too long I had allowed myself to be controlled by gratitude. I had to claim my own life back from the person who was living it for me. Once I'd done that, I could look objectively at her and our relationship. There. I'd convinced myself.

Queues in the market sector... A war over the latest puddle of oil discovered in the DeepCore Operations... Rumours that the Hood hierarchy was about to be reshuffled... A Litcrime discovered in one of the Hives on the edge of the city — some fool reciting poetry to an underground audience. He was to be burned publicly in a few hours. I thought of Rouffe and the risks we were taking and shuddered.

Marley had moved on to new ground. My mask was beginning to smell, she said. It wasn't. I peeled it off and showed her how little fluid there was, how clean the scars were. The wires unfurled from the socket of my eye like a questing anemone. I only stopped when she began to cry. I left her and went to the bedroom, knowing full well that nothing would be resolved here. I went out. Fuck the dangers.

I'd never been outside at this hour before. Zeps moved across the sky, a necklace of moons, underlit by the blinking sequins of their beacon mappers as they roved the country, feeding data to the Hoods HQ; the new satellites since cloud cover reached 100 per cent and made all those NASA trinkets up there redundant. I could tell it wasn't going to be easy; the corners of the streets glowed in cones of light and movement; Hoods, or worse, picking off stragglers like me. It was anything goes, this time of night. Flouting curfew rules was as close to committing suicide as you could get. I could imagine the shell from one of the Hood's ArmaPaks thudding into my good eye and switching off the lights for ever. Kind of comforting. So I pressed on, bitterly relishing the panic Marley would be in when she realised I'd gone.

South of KStreet< I lucked upon a stray Hood and winded him with a kick to the balls, coming out of shadow before he had a chance to draw. I dragged him into the dark and, digging my fingers under the masks of bandage, pulled until they were free of his pocked, sodden face. The speech grille was fused with the flesh of his lips and it stank to high heaven when I finally prised it clear. I divested him of his greatcoat (grenades wadded into the utility belt, very tasty) and his piece – nice one, Huebber and Larroche, twelve rounds, semi-automatic: the deadliest thing you could sit in the palm of your hand, barring Marley's tongue, that is – and got myself into Hood mode, gagging on the smell but it was something I had to learn to live with. Better that than to be gagging on my own blood, my chest torn apart thanks to one from the wrong end of one of these Huebbers.

When it looked like my friend was reviving, I slugged him one on the back of the head, watched him deck it, then gave him another by way of a parting shot. I'd just pulled the snood down over my forehead, stepping back on to the main drag, when a coach slewed into the street and bore down on me with its manifold headlights. It swung in close, doors peeling back, and I hopped on board, leaned languidly over one of the handrails, heart beating out an apocalyptic drum solo. I had no choice in the matter. In the recess of the bus, thirty or so Hoods cast me a cursory glance. I nodded to those who delivered a greeting and then returned my attention to the bland streets blurring into ribbons beyond the window. What had I done? What the *hell* had I done? My panic was such I almost started giggling.

We left the city behind. I didn't know where we were going or how likely I was to be exposed; I suppose that depended heavily on the Hood I'd popped. Maybe he was raped, dead and dismembered by now, jumped by the sewage scavengers for meat.

I hoped so. The coach rattled on towards a range of hills. Dawn was an hour or two away but there was already a greenish pallor to the hilltops and suddenly I was back in childhood, going out for a day trip to the seaside; if I turned round now all the Hoods would be eating ice-cream and singing daft songs:

We're off, we're off, we're off in a motor car

Sixty miles an hour and I don't know where we are

And then I saw that the hills weren't hills at all. They were funeral pyres. I remembered the bulletins concerning the poet. As we approached, I saw that we were to be part of a 'military' presence, to keep the crowds in order. The coach slowed at the same time as a crocodile of rags were led out from a bunker, linked with heavy chains so that they resembled a travelling fence of flesh. I recognised Bunce, the condemned poet, being forced through the throngs of observers, who were busy trying to whip up a froth of anger but it was all for the Hoods, who had forced everyone from their beds to watch this. Everyone was trying to outdo each other's pale outrage. Everyone wore expressions of bewilderment. Nobody knew what was going on anymore.

The human chain was brought to a standstill in front of the bonfires, two people to each woodstack. I shivered, despite the rags swaddling my face, thinking of me and Rouffe bound together and torched for our subversive sessions in that strange, forbidden library.

Then things happened quickly. I saw Keri. She was skirting the edge of the crowd near the front, budged into a position by Hoods who had infiltrated the audience and were like pins in an unwieldy structure, keeping it from fragmenting. What were they doing? Forcing her to watch as a warning to her? Was she their prisoner? Had she been since the last time I saw her, in the plaza? I tried to reveal myself to her, to give her a signal, but there were too many people in the way and too many Hoods nearby.

Marley was easy to spot: a wan figure, motionless in the scrum, her hair hidden beneath a cherry-coloured hat I'd bought her after I came out of hospital. It seemed much of the city had been roused from slumber to observe this display of power; a warning to anybody thinking of subverting the current zombified state. Beyond the outermost fringe of attendees, I saw something else that chilled me. Armoured bikes and Hoods weighed down with heavy artillery wrapped high across their chests or slung low over hips. The throaty ripple of the bikes cut across the clamour of voices. Bunce was trying to be heard above the noise as he recited stanzas that were punched with stinging references to freedom, brotherhood and peace. Oh, the Hoods were mightily wounded, I don't think.

There was going to be trouble. The Hoods had obviously been issued a directive to instigate a riot and to fill some bodybags. I moved towards Marley, trying to get her attention, but she just backed off, eyes oscillating between the insignia on my tunic and the heavy ropes that bound the poet and his cohorts. I gripped the Huebber tightly in my pocket. Although I'd been excited to acquire it, the thought I might use any weaponry seemed remote. Now, the possibility that I would have to be seen to turn it on my neighbours was a sickening realism.

The poets were lashed against the pyres; one of the Hoods drove the butt of his rifle into Bunce's mouth, instantly breaking the poet's jaw and causing him to choke on a mixture of blood and teeth; his verses were lost as he sagged against the structure that would soon be consuming him. This time, a genuine roar of protest was released from the crowd, which surged forward. *No*, I wanted to shout, *it's exactly what they want*. But the crowd had found its strength, its sense of unity. Bonded like this, how could they be denied? Bunce was moving against the wood; a slow, fluid dance as he bucked in his choking fit. His face had turned blue, a great rope of bloodied spittle hung from his shattered jaw. I couldn't see anything but white in his bulging eye sockets.

The Hoods nearest the tide of bodies obviously felt the crowd's charge was provocation enough and emptied their cartridges, point blank. Thirty dead, instantly. I tried moving behind the front line of Hoods to reduce the threat of my involvement but new ranks were forming at my back; I was pressed forward. It was almost comic, the way my path and that of Marley's, were converging.

"Mow them down," said a voice, gritting in my ear like shale against tin.

"What?" I said, trying not to laugh at the poetry of the moment. Bunce was dead, toppled over against his bindings, his face black. The other Litcrims were screaming or remaining stock-still, trancelike, as though by forcing their conscious selves elsewhere they would avoid the pain of their deaths. "Did you say 'Mow them down?'" Marley was two feet away from my unholstered gun, her eyes darting over the disintegrating crowd and the wisps of smoke now rising from the bonfires.

The Hood inclined his head towards me, as though scenting a rat. "Strafe," he said. "Mow. The. Fuckers. *Down.*"

I looked at Marley. I could tell her to run, but then we'd both be dead. Hoods ganged up either side of me. If I didn't act soon...

I had no choice.

Marley fell apart like slow-cooked lamb from the bone. The Hood at my side, toting his Huebber like it was turning to molten metal in his fist, blasted three more people before the crowd jinked my way, spilling us all to the floor. I scrambled out of the stampede, mere feet away from one of the blazing pyres, its human fuel arching against the wood, a blackened twist. I didn't feel the heat at all; cold lead replaced my bones. I did for the Hood who'd wasted Marley, loosing a shell into the bastard's throat; in the confusion, nobody noticed. I spun away, tearing the rags from my face. Keri was being buffeted between pockets of violence like a steel ball in a game of bagatelle. I grabbed her wrist and she resisted until she saw who I was. We legged it over to the van that had brought the condemned prisoners to their execution site. The driver took off out of his seat when he saw me flash the gun at him and I took the controls, Keri settling into the seat behind me, bracing herself against the handrails as I slewed the bus in a tight arc away from the riot. There was a fierce smell of sweat and shit hanging in the bus but I couldn't work out whether it was the fear we were producing or those who had been passengers just a short while ago.

"We being followed?" I yelled above the din of the engine.

"Not that I can see," she shot back. In the mirror she was a tensed white statue, arms marbled with blueish veins, head turned from me as she scanned the back window. Her hair collected in the snood like scoops of toffee. Her tummy formed a smooth border between her tunic and combat trousers, a glass bracelet circling her waist hinting at vanity, glinting as light caught its buffed green surfaces. I grinned, glad that I'd been able to rescue her.

And then I thought of Marley and pretty soon I was thinking of my parents and I had to pull over and let her drive the rest of the way.

We ditched the bus on YWay< and ran to Concrete Park. The adrenaline squirting through me wouldn't allow me to be as stealthy as I might, although it took a while to kick in. I felt hobbled by fear. Too much like the guerrilla campaigns we trained for in Petal Dawn. At least Keri seemed alert enough for both of us. It seemed peaceful enough though, and we managed to spot the few sentries left on duty before running into them.

"Why have we stopped?" asked Keri.

"I'm looking for something."

"What?"

"A way in." Frantically, I scanned the wall, looking for a clue as to the door's current position. I couldn't see it. And I couldn't relax enough to let my eyes absorb the colours and find the edges I was desperate to see. "Shit! Rouffe! *Rouffe*! It's me, Cloake. Open the fucking door!"

What if he'd gone? What if—

Keri's hands clasped my shoulders. She kissed me fully on the mouth, dragging the tip of her tongue along my lips as though looking for her own access. "Calm... down... Cloake," she said, in between deep breaths. "Someone'll hear you. Relax."

She drew me into the shade afforded by a shattered ledge of concrete where dried curls of dog shit and treacly hypos were mashed together; the detritus of some bizarre ritual. My breathing was hot and ragged; she was absently stroking the bulge of my crotch through my fatigues. It didn't promote any sexual warmth, just the comforting pressure I needed to bring myself back down to Earth.

"Better?" she asked.

"Yeah," I said. "Thanks."

"Who's Rouffe?"

I peered out from the wedge of darkness, dividing my attention between looking for Hood activity and trying to crack the codes of Rouffe's chimerical wall. "He's a friend of mine, got a place where we can hide. For a little while at least."

"So let's go."

"In a moment. I've, uh, lost the key to his door."

Then I had it. The swirl of colour seemed to dim and step back from the door, which was projected in glorious 3-D Technicolor. It was as obvious as a wart on a nose.

"Cloake!" Rouffe barked, as I passed through the door. "My, but you look positively riven! Aw, no matter. I have something for you."

Keri moved past me and Rouffe froze.

"Ah," he said.

"Rouffe," I held out my hand, a gesture of conciliation. "I had no choice."

"So it appears. Well, I was getting tired of life. Better come in, I have a pot brewing. I take it you'll share a cup with me?"

We went into his study, where the Oldstuff spilled from their containers like unearthed treasure.

"So this is your Gallery find?" said Rouffe, handing out drinks. "Is she worth all the palaver? I certainly hope so. What does Marley—"

"Marley was killed this morning," I said. "At the execution. There were a lot of deaths."

"I heard about the riots," Rouffe murmured. "I'm sorry." He clapped his hand on my knee and passed me a parcel secured with twine. Keri watched with the silent fascination a cat affords a spider. Her fingers moved across the band around her waist. Its colour had changed. Blue now.

I unwrapped the brown paper, trying to get my brain around the fact that, a few hours prior to this placid, homely act, I'd been firing bullets into skulls.

A teacup chinked in its saucer.

"My God," I said.

The book's dust jacket depicted a white matchstick figure pointing a gun at the reader. Exiting the barrel was the squared off snout of a juggernaut, headlamps blazing. The title, *Long Vehicle*, screamed across the top of the book in red block capitals while the author's name was a sober thread of lower case letters on the juggernaut's registration plate: *Saxon Cloake*.

I turned the book over and the photograph staring out at me snatched the breath from my lungs. Everything blurred over.

"My God," I said again, just for the hell of it.

"I knew you'd be pleased," said Rouffe.

I looked up at him and smiled, hugging the book to my chest. Then there was a sighing noise, which grew louder and didn't stop until a blinding white light filled the room. When I looked up again, I was covered in rubble, my hands scorched black. Rouffe was still sitting in his chair but something wasn't right. His hands gripped the armrests, his immaculately shod feet pointed towards me. But there was hair all over his face. I picked myself up, tensed for any great shocks of pain, and picked my way over to him. In the near distance I heard voices of intent.

I realised my moment of madness, even as I tried to twist his head back into the right position. His tongue lolled almost to his shirt collar. The discs of bone in his neck, as I moved him, ground together: the sound of a pepper mill in use. Books burned; microcosms of life snuffed out.

A shell fizzed past my ear, whining off a butte of granite six feet away.

"Keri!" I called. She was buried, or blown apart. I didn't have time to search for her.

As I made for the far end of Concrete Park, now strewn with chunks of its namesake, I spotted the shattered trinket that had encircled Keri's waist. I snatched it up, bracketed by explosions, and fled into the coming night, trying to pay more attention to my escape route than the lozenges of microcircuitry that spilled from its casing.

It's another beautiful day in the Metropolis. If it weren't for the cloud cover, the sun would be buoying spirits all over town. My hands are healing nicely; I've been wrapping them in DermSynth tissue for the past week. The burns caused quite a bit of damage to the nerves in my fingers but I can still turn the pages of Dad's book. Returning to Marley's dorm seemed like a bad idea, but I had nowhere else to go. As it turns out, I've been unmolested. It looks like I beat them, gave them the slip. Hooray for guerrilla training. There's spirit in this old vet yet.

It was good, Dad's book. I liked the characters and the plotline. There was a very beautiful passage around a third of the way through, when the protagonist loses someone dear to him and he knows that, but for a different course of action, he might have rescued her. He remembers some words she said to him, from the first time they made love.

"If I never knew you, I would never have known what happy meant. And if I ever lost you, it wouldn't be so bad, because I'd have you still, a little warm spot inside me, for ever."

Mawkish, maybe, but I cried a lot when I read that. Gummed my mask up pretty bad. Because I recalled, through the fog of childhood and the blackness of the last few years, that he'd once said those words to me. Leaning over me as he tucked me up in bed, smoothed a hand across my forehead. *If I never knew you...*

So, it's a beautiful day. I think I'll chance a walk. Make sure I've got everything I need. The Chute spits me out and I stroll to DWay>. I press my key against the disc of metal and the partition sinks out of sight; I hurry across its socket and wave at Halve as I approach the iceberg of her desk. She's wearing a black bouclé wool-mix belted shift dress. I know because Marley bought one, last time we went to the Bead. It still hangs, like a spinster suicide, in her wardrobe.

Halve sweeps a delta wave of hair from her eyes. "Catalogue?"

I can hear the fans and the subterranean burble of power. I glance over to the Gallery entrance and there's a shadow retreating from the archway.

"I'll have whatever's on at the moment," I say.

"That'll be '21st century post-coercive intra-narrative faction'," she says, and can't even smile about it.

I'm cooling down as I slip by the uniformed goons and stride over the threshold. Her snood's drawn up around that wheaten mass of hair. In the front of my jacket I've got Dad's book and a grenade, which I triggered before leaving. My hands have been burned so senseless I can't tell one from the other. She doesn't turn round as I approach.

"Cloake," she whispers, staring into a smear of words, "I'm only upholding the law. Why can't this be enough for you? I'll have to report this meeting. You've committed a Litcrime."

We stand there for a little while, watching the meaningless ebb and flow of words pared down to their passionless bones. I slip something into her pocket and walk away. One of us has a reason why. One of us has ten seconds left.

I hope it's me.

Dave's Dinosaur
Peter Borg

"Dave, there's a dinosaur outside!"

Dave opened his right eye a crack, just enough to see the outline of his girlfriend Sarah. He was never at his best first thing in the morning, in fact Sarah had nicknamed him 'The Grumpy Badger' after a children's book she had adored as a child. The Grumpy Badger was not being helped by this strange talk of dinosaurs.

He rolled over and made it clear that he was going to go back to sleep, but Sarah was insistent.

"Dave, I'm not kidding, when I was coming back form the toilet block I saw... I saw... something. It looked liked a Komodo Dragon only it walked upright and it was massive." Sarah continued to shake Dave but it was the way her voice cracked on the word 'massive' that finally got his attention. It sounded very much like she was trying to hold back tears, trying to hold it together. In fact, despite her talk of dinosaurs and all the shaking, she seemed to be trying not to alarm him.

Or, it might possibly have been the bestial, primeval roar that shook the tent, the ground and set off all the car alarms in a three mile radius. Either way, one of these things convinced him that something was seriously amiss.

Dave sat up and his head darted from side to side in a decent impression of a meerkat. He located the direction of the fading roar and stared, almost as if he could see through the material of the tent.

"Dave, what are we going to do?" Dave was thinking exactly the same thing. He didn't really think phoning the police would help. They would be more inclined to laugh at him than help. Even if they did take him seriously he didn't think there was enough police in the world to 'kettle' the thing that made that roar.

He looked at Sarah and noticed her pale face, the tears falling silently from her chin and the tiny bit of toothpaste she had left in the corner of her mouth. He opened his arms and she fell into them, he squeezed tight.

"It's going to be all right," he said, telling the biggest lie since Nick Clegg said he would never raise student fees. "I'm going out to take a look." Dave began wriggling out of his sleeping bag but Sarah started getting even more distressed.

"You can't go out there, Dave, it's huge, it will–" But the rest of her sentence was lost in another bestial roar, this one sounding even closer.

"Sarah, if that thing wants us, I can't really see that three millimetres of tent material are going to help us out that much."

Dave unzipped the tent door and looked back at Sarah. He smiled at her and said once more, "It'll be all right." He winked just as a reptilian clawed arm plucked him from the tent.

The morning sun dazzled Dave and, even though the dinosaur lifted him up to eye level, Dave was only able to make out the silhouette of a huge reptilian head. The dinosaur's arm held him around the waist almost tenderly. Dave shut his eyes as the head lurched forward, so close the skin of a nostril brushed against his face and he felt the dinosaur's warm fetid breath caress his skin. Still he could see no detail of the creature that held him, no idea of the colour or texture of its skin except for the arm, a bright green snake-like limb. He felt and heard, rather than saw, the dinosaur's mouth open and then he heard a sniffling sound, similar to the sounds his old golden retriever made when looking for a chew toy.

Dave felt that was an association he could have done without. He braced himself for death. He realised his life had flashed before his eyes, that was what living was all about, and now, the final scene was to be the snapping of massive jaws. He did take some solace in the fact that this method of death, eaten by dinosaur, was almost certain to make the front page of the local paper. In fact, this story might go national.

Suddenly the dinosaur paused and shifted its grip on Dave's torso then flung him away. Dave cartwheeled through the air, the sky and ground rotating around him, until he landed with a crash a few metres away from the tent door. The green material of the tent framed Sarah's head; she looked freaked out. As he slid to a halt, Dave looked at her and smiled.

"I told you it would be all right," he said. Then it all faded to black.

An Interstellar Taxi Ride
David Ball

Seymour Niples made a deliberate cough in protest at the space-taxi driver's cigarette. Then he made several more coughs, each increasing in their volume until the driver got the hint and put the cigarette out.

Seymour was an Ambassador; he was used to the best things that the galaxy had to offer. He liked fine wines from across the cosmos, and ate from restaurants that served the most exotic and tasty meals in the universe. Seymour removed a silk handkerchief from his impeccably clean dinner suit, and used it to fan away the smoke.

The universe was very large, and heavily populated. It had many methods of travelling between planets, and not all of them were as glamorous as an intergalactic starship. The cheapest option was public transport, which meant travelling with a large number of other offworld travellers. Seymour cringed at the thought of being crammed into a small space with a hundred aliens, each with potentially a different form of alien bacteria or disease that might get sneezed over him.

Or the second cheapest was by space-taxi. Seymour looked around and surveyed the vehicle he was in. It had fake leather wipe-clean seats, which were a little sticky. He was doing his best not to sit on them by spreading his copy of the *Galactic Times* over the seat before he sat down. The floor was littered with bits of food, and drink cans that rolled around spilling their last few drops every time the driver made a quick turn to avoid a meteor, or fellow spacecraft that he somehow hadn't managed to see in the vast void of space in front of them until the very last minute.

It was one of these sudden turns that almost made Seymour slide off his newspaper-covered seat.

"Do you mind?" he said angrily. "I'm desperately trying not to touch anything in this filthy vehicle you call a space-taxi, and you're making it extremely hard for me to do so."

"Sorry pal!" the driver called from the front. "But there was this large comet in the way. I had to do a quick turn to avoid it."

"That comet has been the only thing in front of us for twenty minutes, I'm sure you had plenty of time to see it coming," Seymour said, just quietly enough for it to be drowned out by the noise of the space-taxi's straining antimatter engine.

This wasn't Seymour's first choice of transport of course. He would have loved a Luxury Hyper-Limousine, or just a fully automated Stasis Shuttle, where he could have fallen into a deep sleep and been woken up on his arrival. Although any method of transport would have been acceptable as long as he didn't have to talk to any member of the public. A robot would have done, at least robots don't try to engage you in small talk. They just get the job done. Although there was that time when one tried to kill him, which had put Seymour off robots for a bit. But the reason he was taking this filthy space-taxi was that the transport he'd ordered seemed to have fallen into a black hole, and he didn't have another expenses form to order another. Also, the space port he'd been waiting at was festering with members of the general public which he despised, and he didn't want to wait there a moment longer. He'd looked for any method of transport off that planet and begrudgingly got in this filthy, rickety taxi. At the time he thought it might be a bit of an adventure to 'slum it' and travel like a normal person, he even considered writing a book on it.

Unfortunately the driver of this space-taxi was not a robot, he was a genuine live Human, and was trying to engage him in conversation. Seymour had ignored the driver's two previous attempts, by pretending to be interested in something out of the window, and then pretending to read the ingredients on a packet of cheese and onion crisps. This time the crisp packet was out of reach, and there was nothing out of the window apart from the dull blackness of space.

"So what do you do, pal?" asked the driver, partly turning

around.

Seymour made eye contact, and then immediately wished he hadn't. Now the driver knew for definite that he'd heard him.

"I'm an Ambassador," Seymour said. Normally Seymour would love talking about himself, but in his current surroundings he wasn't much in the mood for anything apart from getting to his destination as fast as possible.

"Oh yeah, pal, what does that mean then?"

What does that mean? What the hell did the driver mean by that? Did he really not know what an Ambassador did? Seymour scoffed rudely.

"It means that I'm very important," he said, and gazed out of the window. He thought this would put a stop to the driver's conversation, but he carried on. He seemed genuinely interested.

"Oh right, wow pal. That's great for you. So do you go to like, posh dinner parties and that then?"

Seymour rolled his eyes. "I have met the greatest leaders of the most important planets in the galaxy. I have shared fine bottles of wine with Kings and Queens of other solar systems, and I have conversed in great detail with Presidents, Prime Ministers and Emperors of more than a hundred other worlds."

"Oh that must be nice for you, pal," the driver said. "You must be a pretty important guy."

Seymour liked to think so, but this was quite exaggerated.

"I think you're the second most important person I've had in this cab," the driver said.

Seymour was gazing out of the window wishing he was on any one of the planets they were passing, rather then being involved in this conversation, until what the driver said registered in his mind.

"Only the second?" Seymour sounded appalled.

"Oh yeah, pal."

Seymour looked around, and couldn't imagine many people

choosing to travel in this moving filth pit.

"May I ask whom?"

"It was Tiffany. Y'know Tiffany Oombits?"

Seymour had to think about it before an image of her came into his mind. "You mean—"

"Yeah, Tiffany Oombits, the supermodel with the three breasts. Man she is hot. You should have seen her, pal."

Seymour rolled his eyes. Every other male in the galaxy seemed to have a thing for Ms. Oombits. She had a third breast which originally made people think she was from some exotic alien planet, until it was revealed that it was a surgical implant for attention, and she was actually from Rotherham in Yorkshire. But even after that, she retained her fans who just thought it made her 'easier to relate to'. She regularly appeared on magazine covers, and adverts for space-age galactic lingerie. Sometimes Seymour felt like he was the only sane person in the galaxy. How dare this space-taxi driver assume she was more important than him?

"Yeah, she sat right there where you are sitting now, pal."

Seymour looked around the cramped space in the back. "As opposed to where?" he said, but the driver ignored him and continued.

"She was with her boyfriend. Or one of many." He chuckled. "They were being all romantic, kissing and cuddling, and they pulled that blind down for some privacy." Seymour's eyes bulged as he waited for the driver's next sentence. "I haven't had the heart to wash the seat since."

Seymour leaped up off the seat in disgust. "Are we nearly there yet please?"

The driver checked his navigation computer and shook his head. "Still a long while off yet, pal."

Seymour spread out more newspapers and sat on the edge of the seat with his arms wrapped around his knees.

"So tell me about your job, pal?" the driver said. "Who do you work for?"

Now this was something Seymour did like talking about. "I work for Her Royal Highness Queen Brittany the first, Queen of England, The United Kingdom and the Commonwealth." He said with his nose in the air.

"Blimey, pal," the driver said. "Queen Brittany? Really?"

Seymour nodded. "I am Royal Ambassador to Her Royal Highness, my duties–"

"Queen Brittany, the hot one that did that nude photo shoot a few years back?"

Seymour sighed. "Her Majesty has done many things in the past few years–"

"But she did that photo shoot though didn't she? She has these cracking..." He moved his hands off the flight sticks and waved them in front of his chest.

"Including a nude photo shoot, yes. It was for charity."

"Yeah, pal, but oh man. It was the best thing ever. I mean, move over Tiffany Oombits, who needs three breasts when you've got such... royal beauties?"

Seymour shifted on his seat uncomfortably. He was well aware that Queen Brittany was an incredible flirt, and he was constantly amazed at how people could forget hundreds of years of proud royal traditions when one of the young royals happens to take her clothes off.

"Hold on, pal, I think I've still got the magazine she was in. I kept it for... a special occasion. Yeah." The driver started looking in a drawer under his navigation computer.

"Please, could you keep your eyes on the flight path. It looks like there is a comet forty minutes in front of us, I don't want us to hit it."

"Yeah, don't worry, pal. The navigation computer will work it out for me."

This made Seymour blink in surprise. If the navigation computer could pilot this spaceship, what was this driver for?

The driver waved the magazine in front of Seymour's face, making him look away bashfully. "Yes. Yes, I see it. Thank you. I don't need to be reminded of it again thank you very much."

"Oh. And she's in this one." The driver pulled out another magazine. "And this!"

Seymour sighed deeply. The Royal family had declined in popularity since the 20th Century, and this had been the first sovereign in over two hundred years that was actually popular with the people. If only it were for the right reasons, Seymour thought.

Obsolete
Christopher Barker

DAPHNE

He lived in a house near the centre of town whose fascia was in a total state of disrepair. Cracks grew through the rendering causing it to crumble and fall to the floor; moss grew about the place indifferently and, in some areas, almost completely carpeted the paving. All this was capped off menacingly by the wrought iron bars across the windows. The back, however, was a different story.

The back garden was the euphoric canvas of a keen gardener with too much time on his hands. Resplendent with all the finer colours of summer; a wide array of blooms bordered a lawn that was roughly eleven foot by ten foot, and were set against a wall of green at least ten feet tall.

What looked like one large wall consuming plant in fact consisted of around fifty large wall crawlers that ran around the entire walled edge of the garden. Over the years they had grown and tangled together and almost become one.

A stepping stone path ran diagonally across the grass and along it shuffled Daphne Tramp, a gentleman of advancing years.

If you were to look upon him that day, Daphne Tramp, hobbling about his garden; if you were to have seen his walk marred by a slight hunch; if you had spied him pottering about his garden both figuratively, and literally, moving the assorted flowers into cheap plastic pots and then replacing them with other flowers just as pretty as the last but younger and just about to burst forth; if you'd have seen him on this hot summer day, wearing a towel draped over his head held in place by a visor, you would have made the assumption that he was getting too old for gardening.

His range of movement these days was becoming more limited.

The moment he forgot about this and exerted himself, his body would remind him with a pulled muscle or an aching bone. Across his heavily shadowed face he wore marks of his past, his forehead wrinkled and his features strained, a bead of sweat dripped from his large hooked nose and dropped to the soil.

He was originally of Greek descent, a fact belied by his avoidance of the sun. He hated it, the sunshine made his bones creek, but he would always grin and bear it.

He barely even felt it today though, the pain, the heat. Spending time thinking about the flowers and concentrating on them left no room for other, more sinister thoughts that plagued him.

As a young man he always said that looking behind was hardest because it was unnatural, the neck shouldn't bend like that, and the only way to see it was to turn your back on the future. He used to think it was a witty and amusing analogy but the future was so bleak now he couldn't help but crane his neck.

He thought of Julie and Ben, he thought only of their names as their faces had escaped him long ago.

The doorbell rang; the shrill noise carried through the house and spilled into the garden, stealing his attention away from his flowers. He stirred from his kneeling position, slowly but purposefully, and got to his feet. Ignoring the twinge of 'old-age' in his knee, he started towards the house, passing his cat on the way.

"I really need to teach you to answer the door one of these days, Mendel." He didn't wait for a reply.

Daphne knew who it was at the door before opening it.

Once a week, he would receive a few boxes of food, drink and other necessities to last him until the next. Daphne had no working timepiece but was reasonably sure it must be around 2.00 pm, unless they had changed the delivery time, but that would be very unlike the military.

Since he was never allowed to leave the house the food was delivered to him, and the delivery boy, out of fear as much as under orders, never spoke to him or acknowledged his existence to any great degree. There was no signing of forms or exchanging of money, he would just carry in the boxes to the small kitchen and then leave, picking up the boxes from last week's delivery as he went. Daphne would always greet him with a friendly "Hullo!" all the same.

The delivery boy entered as usual, set the boxes in their place and left in all of roughly six minutes, Daphne's "Bye!" left hanging in the air, cut-short by the slamming of the door as he stood alone once more.

"Are they getting younger or is it just me?" Mendel was tongue-tied; all he could do was meow and stretch.

The parcels themselves contained a variety of food and drink, tin cans, bottles and boxes all stacked and arranged very efficiently. Not once in all the years he'd been here had he ever received a broken or damaged item. Also, not once in all these years had the packaging on the items ever changed in design; not that there was much to the design to be changed. Each item, whether in a tin or a bottle or a box, had as its label black text in some sort of stencilled font, on a white background. There was no nutritional information or pictures, just the name of the item in large bold text.

As per his routine he put all the items away in their place on the shelves of his cupboards and then he would flatten the boxes and place them by the door ready for next week. All that remained was for him to finish his work in the garden and then retire to bed.

BLOOMSDAY

Daphne sprung up in his bed suddenly.

His mechanical alarm clock made an awful din as the big hand pointed to twelve and the little to six. His internal alarm clock protested furiously.

He stopped the noise and rubbed his eyes in an effort to get his brain moving, he never got up this early... then he remembered.

He pivoted on his rear end and swung his legs out of his huge four-posted bed. Dressed only in his nightshirt, he ran to the window, almost tripping on the corner of the bed, and cursed under his breath. He flung back the curtains excitedly and was hit by the light from the sun that had just cleared the buildings around him. He looked down to the garden below, craning his neck for a better view of what he was looking for, until his head bumped against the cold glass.

"Today is the day, Mendel!" Mendel opened his left eye, watched Daphne leave, then closed it again and rolled over lazily. On his way to the stairs, Daphne grabbed a pair of trousers and a fleece from the laundry basket, his knees screamed out as he tried to high step his way into the corduroys and run at the same time.

He passed his large grandfather clock, that he had long ago stopped, to rid himself of its incessant ticking, and caught his reflection, making a mental note to remember to shave today.

He went via the kitchen and through the back door leaving it gaping behind him. He almost skipped down the stones that led across the lawn to the soil that bordered the garden.

There in the soil; flanked on both sides by all sorts of plants, climbing and ground alike, stood a wooden cylinder, roughly four inches in diameter. It stood on its end, around a foot tall, and on the top end there was thin glass. He looked through this little window and gasped. Slowly he lifted the cylinder up revealing the prize below.

He touched one of the three flowers gently and moved his shaking fingers deftly around and through perfectly formed white and yellow petals. Imagine the markings of a cow but instead of black there was yellow and this was what enraptured him presently. He rocked backwards and came to rest on his bottom, arms spread out wide behind him for support, and just gazed at the flowers.

A chorus from some feeding birds in the corner of his garden stirred him from his reverie; standing slowly, he barely took his eyes from the flowers until the last moment.

His shed was large with room to sit and do things in shade and comfort. Lining the walls were a selection of tools, some obviously more used than others. He looked around and clicked his tongue against the roof of his mouth, a habit he had when thinking. The clicking stopped and he pulled open a draw. There was a brief, dull clang as the contents slid and collided with one another. He reached in and retrieved a pair of small pruning clippers and returned to the flowers, leaving the shed door open.

His hands paused close to the flowers; they were shaking now more than ever. Slowly, his left hand manoeuvred around the stem, being careful, trying to avoid the thorns. Then, it moved back sharply as a thorn gave him a small prick, which barely drew blood. He sucked his thumb dry and made another attempt. His right hand drew in, clasping gently, as he snipped a little less than midway up the stem of that one flower and laid it to one side.

He grasped the second, this time there was no accidental prick; he snipped it in roughly the same place and laid it down next to him; his movements were slower now and less sure, as if he was contemplating the merits of his next intended moves.

Whatever his precise thoughts, the debate was settled quickly. He wrapped the two roses individually in tough waxed paper and carried them carefully.

After a quick trundle around the house, he stood in the middle of his kitchen peering about for anything he might have missed. He had his shoes on and a hat, his favourite deerstalker that had gotten him through years of... well everything but stalking deer.

He looked left and right in case there was anything he had forgotten, then picked up the flowers and made his way to the front door.

CLICK

The door was locked from the outside, even after all these many years they were still efficient in remembering to lock the door after themselves.

It was no good trying the windows, they were reinforced bullet-proof glass and could only be opened a sliver to allow air to circulate. His shoulders slumped dejectedly, the cat meowed at his feet and rubbed against his shins, a smile forced its way out.

He let out a shrug then a sigh and walked into the kitchen talking absently to his cat.

"Silly Daphne—" he berated himself, "...silly, foolish Daphne."

He lay the flowers down and leant arms astride on the countertop looking out the window across the garden. He stared at the one remaining rose, the estranged sibling of the two flowers that lay upon his table top. His eyes wandered around the contours, the whole backyard seemed to be surrounded by plants, so dense that the wall behind wasn't visible. Maybe there wasn't one there, he thought to himself. He recalled there being one, but couldn't really trust his memory. As he gazed absently, he imagined bursting through the foliage and emerging on the other side.

He walked out taking his flowers with him and paced around the edges of the garden, feeling the plants delicately. After visiting the shed again for the pruning scissors, he snipped and pulled at sections to test them.

Slowly and methodically he worked his way along the perimeter snipping some choice branches and then pulling in the hope that something would give. They weren't giving way and were attached to the wall quite solidly but he continued on until, eventually, he thought he felt the foliage shift and give.

He tried again; he definitely felt it this time. He dropped the pruning shears to the floor and took the branches with both hands; after a silent three count, he yanked with all his might.

The foliage gave way, in part revealing an old, black and moss-covered gate set into the wall. His heart leapt, and the ache in his bones faded, as he tore away the remaining vines and examined the gate.

It was a sturdy gate, however the lock had rusted quite substantially; again he retreated to his shed and clicked his tongue against the roof of his mouth. He tested different tools in his head before deciding. He took the rake from its hook and hurried back to the gate. Standing a slight way back from it, he hoisted the rake above his head and swung it, bringing the pointy end down in an arc. There was a clang and the lock came apart slightly. He swung again and the padlock came clean off. He dropped the rake and stepped forward, his heart beating faster now as he paused at the gate. His hand gripped the handle tightly; it all seemed so close now, this is what he wanted, but it scared him. When would he be back? Who would feed Mendel?

He swallowed deeply, firmed his resolve, before opening the gate and, with no hesitation, stepping through into the world beyond.

OBSOLETE

Daphne stood dumb founded.

He didn't know what he had expected to see but he knew this wasn't it. Time had moved so quickly during his years of solitude. His body stuttered forward of its own accord, he caught himself and turned to close the door behind him, worried about someone entering his jail cell whilst he was away.

It was then he noticed the stencil, on the outside of the door in that distinctive broken font, the same font as the lettering on his weekly rations, was the word 'Obsolete.' The word held him for a moment before dumping him back into the world with a bump.

"Sorry," muttered the figure whose shoulder had just collided with his. He pulled his coat close to steel his nerves before he plunged into the undulating masses.

As he stepped rapidly through the crowd, dodging and shuffling alternately, he noticed that the buildings he recognised seemed different. Sure the signs were brighter, simpler, but there was something more. All the buildings around him seemed smaller. The shops that he recognised from his youth were dwarfed by a giant structure a few streets over that grew above the rooftops ahead. It seemed to be made entirely of glass; a far away sky reflected in its panels giving an eerie illusion of transparency.

Daphne jostled once again, buffeted by another figure disappearing as quickly as the last. He pushed aside the doubts that began to creep in and continued down the road that was set on a decline. He reached the intersection with the high street. He paused for a moment to get his bearings and his mind overlaid an image of the high street as he remembered it.

Things seemed wrong though. The busy vibrant part of the high street should have been to his left but it was to his right that was getting all the traffic, up towards the huge structure he had noticed earlier. It was almost as if the whole city had shuffled along over the years, slowly, like he shuffled through his garden. Daphne's destination though lay to the left, the road less travelled as usual.

He strolled along, thankful that the crowds were thinner here. He pictured the greeting card shop, the fast food restaurant, and the fashionable designer outlet, none of which existed now.

What had once been a vibrant, loved part of so many lives now was abandoned and forgotten. Like him, it was left behind by time and society. Obsolete.

He remembered walking with Ben one Saturday long ago, his son pointing at the large cut out of a long forgotten icon in the video game store, noticeable now by its dark interior and 'FOR LET' signs in the window.

A sharp pain bit into his palm, the retaliation of a thorn that had pressed through the wax paper attempting to escape his tightening grip. He swapped the blooms into his other hand and carried on, passing a group of youths walking in the opposite direction.

One of the group pointed at him and the rest laughed in unison. He couldn't help feeling apprehensive but couldn't place why. Back in his day they had young people too, but these ones exuded an air of menace and it shook him up.

Daphne's instincts cried out, telling him to return to his 'cage.' He ignored them and ploughed on to the traffic lights where he crossed carefully, but there were no cars or buses here either.

The further he wandered the fuzzier things became. Only one piece of this end of the high street was familiar to him, it jumped out and, for the first time since he left his garden, it felt like the world he knew.

WHOSE VAULT WAS IT?

'The Vaults' resided in what used to be a series of underground catacombs. To enter he had to manoeuvre his stiff joints down a set of narrow steps. He couldn't remember them being this steep before, and he had to stop halfway down. His knees screamed out and he clutched the flimsy railing to support himself.

Foolish old man! Don't come this far just to break your goddamn hip.

The interior of the bar had changed a lot since the last time he was here. All around different machines hugged the wall. One amused him in particular, it sold cigarettes and was directly under a 'no smoking' sign. Another he guessed was a jukebox; however it was small enough to be mounted on the wall. There was also the addition of a wafer thin TV suspended in the corner; he assumed that the rest was buried in the wall.

His gaze fixed finally on the bar, the faint unnatural blue glow from behind rows upon rows of spirits turned his stomach. Bright card cut-outs shouted their offers.

'2 pints for £2, 5 mystery shots for £4.'

Thankfully there were a few familiar pumps lining the counter, at which a young girl in a tight black top and piercings stood expectantly.

"What can I get you?"

The question somehow stumped him and he looked at her chest without meaning to. He had been looking for a name badge, but since when had barmaids worn badges? All those years spent in the house with no female interaction had made him forget how pleasing breasts were to look at. What he had read on her near perfect breasts made him uncomfortable.

'Just show me your cock and we'll call it even!'

"What – do – you – want – to – drink?" She strained each word, slowing them down, making him feel stupid.

He quickly looked at the pumps making sure to control his wandering eyes; at random he picked one of the ales by virtue of the picture on it.

"Go-Golden Harvest, please."

The girl took a glass from some hidden alcove beneath the bar and began to pump the handle. Her hands expertly tipped the glass and eased it upright as the light amber liquid filled the glass, a thin head forming and covering the top of the glass.

"That's two thirty-four please." She placed the pint in front of him and he froze.

He patted his pockets down knowing full well he didn't have any money, maybe some would appear though.

"Oh, I err..." His words dragged, he felt tired all of a sudden. "I don't, err. I don't have–"

"This one's on me!"

Daphne thought he had imagined that voice a moment ago, the barmaid didn't help, her face locked on his. She carried on not acknowledging the phantom voice until it waved a five-pound note beneath her nose.

Even if Daphne had found money in his pocket, he had a feeling it wouldn't have been valid. The colours were more vivid than he remembered, the bills smaller. The barmaid looked at the source of the voice and then took the money without comment, her piercings shifted to emphasise her annoyance.

Daphne turned to his Samaritan; he nodded and mentally slapped himself for being so rude.

"Thank you," he managed to force out.

"No problem." The man's smile reassured Daphne. His body language was open, approachable and made him want to spill all his secrets. Maybe he was a vicar, or a psychiatrist.

"Are you from around here?"

"Sort of..." He worked in his head, took the truth and bent it into something more ordinary. "I used to live here, a long time ago, but I went away for a while."

"And now you're back. That's something to drink to." The man raised his glass and held it there. Daphne got the hint and knocked his glass against the one floating expectantly. "David!"

It took a moment for this to register as an introduction.

"Huh? Oh sorry. Daphne... Daphne Tramp."

David's face froze and Daphne held his breath, had the name been recognised? There was no way it could have been, unless he was now the bogeyman? A cautionary tale told to stop others from making the same mistakes. David eventually cracked.

"Daphne? Really? Isn't that a girl's name?"

"Yes, but it's the one my parents gave me." Daphne took a mouthful of ale and held it between his cheeks for a moment, letting it wash slowly over his tongue on its way to his throat.

"Good?"

"Yes. Thank you. It's been a long time since I've had a pint." He took another sip and savoured the acutely bitter, honey taste.

David examined Daphne over the top of his own glass then, placing it down, he spoke.

"I love the retro kit you're wearing, some of it looks original."

Daphne's cheeks flushed as he realised just how much he stood out amongst the patrons of the bar. Clothes that until a few moments ago had felt quite ordinary now shrunk under the weight of scrutiny. He pulled at the collar letting out some of the hot air that built up beneath his lapels.

"What's in the paper?" The barmaid lifted her chin towards the wax paper bundle he had placed on the bar next to him.

"Flowers." His gaze locked onto the bar top and he stooped to take another swig of his beer.

"Awwwwwww." The corners of her mouth sprung upwards towards her eyes. "You shouldn't have!"

She laughed at her own joke and Daphne felt it rude not to pretend a laugh back.

"Huh. No. They're for my wife and son." He placed his hands on the bundle and stroked it.

"Oops, what did you do?" Her mouth flapped wildly, the words were unthinking, but David seemed to catch the vibes that hung just under Daphne's words and, with a look, cut her impending laugh off.

"For their graves." Daphne looked up from the flowers now to the girl who had frozen in place unsure of what to say, then to David who stared into his glass and was collecting his thoughts ready for the next thing he was going to say. "I'm sorry."

It hardly seemed worth all the planning. He noticed Daphne supping back the last of the liquid from his glass. "Lucy, get me and this gentleman another pint please!"

Glad of the opportunity to be elsewhere, she nodded and bustled to her task.

"I don't have any money to pay you back."

"Don't worry about it, it's on me." Lucy returned with their beers and set them down. David handed her some coins and she turned to the till. "So where have you just come back from?"

"I guess you could say prison." The mixture of alcohol and the gent's sunny disposition crashed through the last of his inhibitions. He heard the words coming from his mouth but couldn't stop them. "Well, more like house arrest."

David struggled to hold his smile as rigid as possible, he thought Daphne might be joking but didn't have the conviction to call him on it.

"What did... or didn't you do?"

Daphne picked up the crack in David's voice.

"Ever heard of 'The Gam'?"

He left the question out there and took a long, thoughtful swig of his beer.

"Yeah, I had it as a child I think. Used to be this big scary disease but nowadays it's curable in a matter of days."

Daphne nodded. "Well I cured that... back when it *was* big and scary."

Out of Daphne's eye-line, Lucy made circular motions with her finger around her ear.

"I was one of Britain's top genetic research scientists when the disease broke out. I was part of the UN task force put together to fight the Gam. The rest of the team were bureaucrats though, they had no idea what had to be done to cure the population. I did though; I worked away in my lab while those ungrateful sods argued amongst themselves."

"You cured the Gam and then were arrested? Forgive me for laughing but..."

Daphne was not laughing. He was more serious now than ever. David trod carefully, "Why would they do that?"

Daphne placed his hand on the wax bundle again; the noise of a bar full of people not saying anything was all around now.

Daphne almost fell from his chair as a voice pierced the silence.

"Why don't you tell him what you did, Daphne?"

A gasp reverberated through the bar. No one had noticed the four heavily armed soldiers who now stood at the entrance to the bar, and the General stood out in front of them. The General, who had spoken previously, stared directly at Daphne. The soldiers, flanking, all held their rifles, pointing down but ready for action.

Daphne righted himself on the stool and clenched his fists. "I cured the Gam." He turned all of a sudden to the rest of the bar. "EVERYONE HERE OWES THEIR LIFE TO ME!"

"But you didn't save everyone, did you, Daphne?"

"Shut up!!"

"You didn't save your wife and son, did you? How did they die again Daphne?"

"SHUT UP!"

"They were sick with the Gam, weren't they, Daphne, but that's not what killed them."

"NO—PLEASE—NO!"

"What killed them Daphne? What killed Ben and Linda?"

"GM241."

"That's right. The 'cure' you were so sure of that you dosed a whole ward of patients with, including your own family!"

David spoke and looked surprised that he had done so. "Isn't GM242 what is given to Gam patients at the moment?"

Although the general's eyes never left Daphne, he answered the question.

"That's right; the Doctor here was one iteration away from being a messiah... one digit away from *not* being a mass murderer."

"I went to the scientific advisory committee that you were a part of, before I did what I did, you turned a blind eye. It's obvious now why, you needed a fall guy."

"Fuck you. We all had family that were affected by the Gam. We all understood your desire to cure it. Do you think you'd still be around if that wasn't the case? Some of the board wanted to have you killed; instead we kept you locked away as a reminder for the future."

Daphne's shoulders sagged and he returned to a hunched position over his pint.

"You bare the weight of a country's guilt on you, Daphne. The country needs you to be locked away. We are a civilised nation, extending compassion even to someone who has committed the crimes you have committed. You understood this once."

"I also used to be able to remember my wife's face... things change." The brief lull of a topic run its course appeared then vanished. "How did you know I had gotten out? I thought I had more time till it was discovered."

"Mendel."

"That two faced snitch, I forgave him for going to the neighbours for food but this is too far."

"In his defence he had no choice, we fitted him with a video camera."

"Where? I would have noticed."

The General pointed to his eye and smiled. Daphne sighed and looked down at the bar.

"Drink your drink and then we are leaving. The garden gate should be bricked up by the time we get back."

"Can we stop at their graves? I have these..."

"No." The reply was short, curt and non-negotiable. All that remained was for Daphne to neck his pint, thank David, and to hobble slowly out, flanked on all sides by the enforcers of his country's penance.

The Smell of Fear
Neal James

This was becoming ridiculous and high time that something was done about it. The neighbourhood never used to be like this until George stuck his pug-ugly nose into everyone's business, and boy was he ugly. A broken leg resulting from a hit and run, a nose spread across his face after a fight in another area and a fearsome cut diagonally from above the right eye to just below the opposite jaw line lent him all the attributes of a real bruiser. Mickey would not have liked to bump into whoever dealt that one out in a dark alley. He shuddered at the very thought of it.

  Nevertheless George had continued undaunted in his terrorism of the streets, and a system of early warning signals had been set up across the neighbourhood in an attempt to forewarn the unwary of his approach. Today was Mickey's lucky day; Scotty had seen the bully turning the corner of Linden Avenue and the word spread like wild fire. Pretty soon the streets were empty as doors were shut tight behind the backsides of fleeing escapees. Anxious faces peeped out from behind a multiplicity of curtains as George's swagger took him down the road like some gunslinger out of Dodge City – you could almost hear the theme from Sergio Leone's 'The Good, The Bad and The Ugly' ringing out in the background. No prizes for guessing which one the bully wasn't.

  He stopped at the corner of Springfield Road and looked back one more time, scanning the bushes and hedgerows for any hidden stragglers who hadn't made it home in time. He snorted his disgust at another day without satisfaction. If things didn't return to normal pretty soon, he'd have to look elsewhere for his entertainment. Yawning long and loud, he finally stomped his way down towards the town's main street and other pickings. Fear has its own particular smell, and the area bore an odour which you could almost taste; it was a taste which George found irresistible.

  Slowly, and with much nervous glancing up and down the street, emerging residents breathed a sigh of relief at another successful daily running of the gauntlet. They all knew that it would only be a matter of time until one poor unfortunate would be caught unprepared, and when that day came all of George's frustration would be meted out indiscriminately to the stranded individual. They needed a plan, not just some imported 'anti-bully' who would then set the area up for himself. No, it would need to be one or more of their own number, and for the sake of permanence they would need to stick together, watching each others' backs in case the retaliation failed to remove the perpetrator for good.

George's initial activities had been restricted to basic needs. He stole whatever food and drink he could from them and had often lain in wait for his victims at street corners. A simple startling was all that had been needed then and he would simply pick up whatever it was that had been dropped. However, as his reputation began to grow and potential victims adopted a more cautious routine, he was compelled to actively seek out his next target. Mickey could cope with running that risk himself, but when the lout picked on Molly it made his blood boil. She was the smallest of the group of friends and quite unable to defend herself against the unwelcome attentions of Ugly George as they had come to call him. Those attentions had also graduated from merely mugging, to ones of a more amorous nature.

Mickey and Molly had lived next door to each other since forever. Growing up so close provided an opportunity for their relationship to develop, and down the years the rest of the group of friends had come to regard them as an item. There was nothing that Mickey wouldn't do for her. George's intrusion into the neighbourhood and the relationship with Molly in particular was the catalyst he needed.

George had a tendency to drool when faced with something particularly tempting, and the thought of him blocking the alleyway where they all usually met when Molly had been caught alone had Mickey in paroxysms of fury. This had definitely been the final straw. That she had been able to escape relatively unharmed was not the point at issue, and it would not take much more reluctance on the part of the rest of them before he committed some far more serious act. A council of war was convened at Robbie's house that night.

George would have to be tackled head on, and one of them would need to be the sacrificial goat. Eight pairs of eyes flitted nervously around the garage where the meeting was held out of the way of prying faces. The silence was deafening and seemed to go on forever. In the end Mickey knew that it would be down to him as unofficial leader of the group, and he sighed as his volunteering was enthusiastically accepted by the rest of them. The relief of the other seven was overwhelming, but Mickey's stomach was now beginning to churn uncontrollably. The matter would have to be dealt with quickly and soon, before anyone got seriously hurt.

The idea was simple; Mickey would 'lie in wait' for George at the mid point of his favourite route and issue the challenge. He closed his eyes and swallowed deeply at the thought of what might be about to happen to him, but summoned up all of his courage and smiled at the rest of the group – it was going to be fine he said. The last thing that a bully wanted was someone standing up to him; in all probability he would simply turn tail and run. 'In your dreams,' Mickey thought to himself, but kept that one from the rest – now was not the time to crush their fragile bravery, he was going to need their back up when the time came.

He didn't sleep much that night, tossing and turning, kicking the blanket off his bed and rising the following morning bathed in a thin film of sweat. Breakfast was not an option, and he was out of the house before anyone else spotted him. It was a Sunday morning and the day for the communal 'lie-in' – for everyone else that is. They were all waiting for him at Robbie's garage and it became clear that no-one had rested at all since the preceding day.

Mickey laid out the details of the plan which had been buzzing around in his head all night, and each member of the group was assigned a position and a specific role. All clearly understood what it was that they had to do. It would only take one slip up and George would be off the hook with God only knows what consequences for the rest of them. As the time ticked inexorably towards midday, Mickey sat with a package on the wall at the end of his yard waiting in a state of heightened tension for the approach of his nemesis. Right on cue the stocky form of George emerged from behind the fence at the top of the street. He slowed his walk as he caught sight of the smaller form standing some thirty yards away. An evil leer spread across his battered face and with his characteristic swagger he bore down upon the defenceless figure now getting closer and closer. He stopped and glared down at his smaller opponent, puffing out his ample chest.

"Mickey. Well, well what a surprise. Caught you napping today have we? Now tell me, what do we have here then?" Nodding in the direction of the ill-concealed bundle.

Snatching Mickey's lunch he took a huge bite out of it in his usual coarse manner. The smile disappeared from his face almost immediately as the tell-tale taste of urine, donated generously by everyone in the group, spread throughout the inside of his mouth. Dropping the remainder of the meal, and with eyes now bulging, he coughed and choked his way into the middle of the street quite unable to make out exactly where he was going. It was the signal for the rest of the action to begin.

From several gateways and concealed hiding places, the remainder of the gang emerged to surround the temporarily incapacitated bully. Mickey moved to the middle of the road to face George as he fought to regain his senses; he grinned at the now pathetic figure as it writhed before him. It was now or never, and if they failed at this point they would suffer for the rest of their lives.

"Now!" Mickey barked out the command, and from every angle teeth and claws descended upon George as he tried in vain to defend himself from the concerted attack.

Mickey had been right in the end. The last thing that a bully expected was someone, much smaller than himself, standing up to his terror tactics. Not only that, George had also badly miscalculated the effects of his regime on a group of close friends. 'Divide and conquer' was all very well with a fragmented opposition, but he had polarised all eight of them into one ferocious and effective unit. He was powerless against the smaller, more nimble and highly motivated squad. Bites and nips were coming in from all angles and with eight sets of claws to deal with, in addition to razor sharp teeth, he took the first opportunity to turn tail and run. Even at the death it was Molly, who had arguably suffered the most unpleasant treatment from George, who got in the final blow.

Latching onto the middle of his tail, she brought a set of crocodile-like teeth clamping down firmly and with enormous force. The squeal of pain brought several householders running from their gardens to investigate. There was, of course, nothing to see by the time they arrived apart from a celebratory lap of honour around the street. As if in tribute to their successful campaign, an ice cream van turned into the top of the road playing its familiar jingle. The tune, as if it could be any other, 'The Good, The Bad and The Ugly' – Sergio would have been proud of them all. George left one reminder of his presence, and the smell of fear which emanated from the pile he deposited was one which they could put up with for now.

News of the humiliation spread like wild fire throughout the district, and stories came back to the group of a number of similar confrontations as other groups of former victims extracted similar acts of vengeance on the now bruised and battered Labrador.

Biographies

Derby Scribes members: -

Alison J. Hill was born in Derbyshire in 1971, and has been writing as a hobby for six years. She has recently had an article published in *Dog's Monthly* magazine, and is currently working on her first novel.

Alison's interests really lie within the film industry in the form of script writing, for which she has begun work on her first film script.

When she isn't writing, Alison is busy bringing up two children and works as a Registered Chiropodist running her own Chiropody business.

Christopher Barker was born in Derby, England in 1982. His published writing to date consists of seven short reviews written for *NEO Magazine* and a handful of short comic stories in various anthologies, including *Murky Depths*.

He also colours and letters comics and has recently been colouring the webcomic *HeroHappyHour.com*.

In the one or two hours that he isn't thinking about, writing, colouring or lettering comics he works for Rolls-Royce; the details of which are too boring for words.

More information about Christopher Barker can be found on his website www.fictionchris.com

David Ball was born in Yorkshire. He has built websites for a living for a company in Derby since 2006.

He likes to write short stories and flash fiction, usually about science fiction. David puts a lot of his writing effort into play-by-post games, which are like interactive stories written by a group of members. His longest running game is *JMC Blue Dwarf*, a space-opera based on the comedy sci-fi series *Red Dwarf*.

David takes a lot of his creative inspiration from sci-fi TV shows. He admits that he doesn't read as much as he should, but does like to listen to story podcasts like *Escape Pod* and *Pseudopod*.

David also runs the website *Ongoing Worlds* www.ongoingworlds.com where you can create and take part in interactive stories.

Jennifer Brown was born in 1982 in the Midlands and has mostly stayed there ever since, though she did briefly manage to escape across the Atlantic at one point. She moved to Derby in 2008 and now spends her working days at Rolls-Royce pretending to know what she's talking about.

Jenn spent years writing fan fiction based on Derby's very own Tomb Raider games but her involvement in Derby Scribes has encouraged her to attempt the daunting task of coming up with something original. Her favourite genres to write are action/adventure with a nice backdrop of drama, but she proudly completed a science fiction piece for Script Frenzy 2010, albeit ten minutes before the deadline.

When she's not writing or working, Jenn is usually exercising, playing video games, watching films or flaunting her powers as a moderator in a Tomb Raider discussion forum.

Peter Borg has enjoyed reading and writing since he could pick up a pen. He mostly wrote fantasy fiction with elements of magic realism but has been known to experiment with all genres of fiction.

He also has a keen interest in stand-up comedy, is currently writing his own routine and trying it out on open-mike sessions.

Peter has just finished studying to be a teacher and hopes to achieve the elusive state of gainful employment sometime soon.

Richard Farren Barber was born in Nottingham, England. After studying in London he returned to the East Midlands. He lives with his wife and son and works as a Development Services Manager for a local university.

He has had short stories published (or due for publication) in *All Hallows, Alt-Dead, Blood Oranges, Derby Telegraph, ePocalypse: emails at the end, Gentle Reader, Murky Depths, Midnight Echo, Morpheus Tales, Scribble, Shriek Freak Quarterly, The House of Horror, This is Derbyshire, Time in a Bottle* and broadcast on *BBC Radio Derby*.

For 2010/11 Richard is being sponsored by *Writing East Midlands* to undertake a mentoring scheme where he will be supported in the development of his novel *Bloodie Bones*. His website *Deadfallonline* can be found at www.richardfarrenbarber.co.uk

Stuart Hughes was born in Burton upon Trent in March 1965. He lives with his wife Margaret in Belper, Derbyshire.

He has had over sixty short story credits in various magazines, anthologies and newspapers, including *Alt-Dead*, the *British Fantasy Society Journal, Dementia 13*, the *Derby Telegraph*, and the collection *Ocean Eyes*.

For nine years he edited *Peeping Tom*, which won the British Fantasy Award in 1991 and 1992.

In addition to the *Derby Scribes 2011 Anthology*, his work has been published this year in the *Alt-Dead* anthology, *Dark Horizons (British Fantasy Society Journal)*, the *Derby Telegraph, ePocalypse: emails at the end, Golden Visions, Midnight Street* and *Sex and Murder*. With further fiction forthcoming in *Dark Horizons (British Fantasy Society Journal)* and *Morpheus Tales*.

A lifelong Derby County supporter, Stuart's Rams related match reports and articles have been published in the *Derby Telegraph* and on the *Derby County Mad* and *RamZone* websites.

His website, *Stuniverse – the world of imagination*, can be found at www.stuarthughes.webs.com

Victoria Charvill is a veteran NaNoWriMo and Script Frenzy participant and knows how to see a project or story through to its completion. She is a Freelance Proof reader and Editor, as well as Editorial Assistant for *Murky Depths*. When not editing, Vicky can be found looking after two kids, a baby, a dog, and painting Warhammer figures.

Guests: -

Alex Davis is a writer, tutor, speaker and events organiser based in Derby. His writing has previously been published in *Dark Horizons, The Harrow, Carillon, SP Quill and Harlequin Magazine* and *Morpheus Tales*. He worked in Literature Development for several years, in this time organizing a range of events, including being involved in Derby's annual Alt.Fiction event, as well as running the first East Midlands Writing Industries Conference and a host of literature festivals.

Alt Fiction: www.altfiction.co.uk

Writing East Midlands: www.writingeastmidlands.co.uk

Conrad Williams is the author of seven novels, four novellas and a collection of short stories. He won the International Horror Guild Award for Best Novel in 2007. He has won three British Fantasy Awards – for Best Newcomer in 1993, for Best Novella in 2008, and for Best Novel in 2010. Conrad was a guest author at Derby Scribes' second writing retreat in June 2008. For more information about Conrad Williams visit his website www.conradwilliams.net

Neal James is a qualified accountant of thirty years' experience.

His first novel *A Ticket to Tewkesbury* was published in October 2008. A collection of his short stories was published in 2009 and his second novel *Two Little Dicky Birds* was published in 2010.

Neal James was a guest speaker at Derby Scribes in September 2010.

For more information about Neal James visit his website www.nealjames.webs.com

Samantha Eynon is a Midlands based artist/illustrator, workshop coordinator, designer, doodler, music lover, VW Campervan owner and paper and vinyl toy enthusiast amongst other things. She is sometimes known by her moniker 'littlegamgee' and has also just launched a new venture with her husband, called *Robots and Rainbows* www.facebook.com/Robots.n.Rainbows. They aim to create awesome T-shirts and other bits and bobs.

Simon Clark is the author of such highly regarded horror novels as *Nailed By The Heart, Blood Crazy, Darker, Vampyrrhic and The Fall*, while his short stories have been collected in *Blood & Grit* and *Salt Snake & Other Bloody Cuts*. He has also written prose material for the internationally famous rock band U2. Simon Clark was a guest speaker at Derby Scribes in February 2011. For more information about Simon Clark visit his website www.bbr-online.com/nailed/

About Derby Scribes

Derby Scribes is a writing group based in the City of Derby.

We currently meet in a private room at the Brunswick Inn, on the first and third Mondays of each month (between 7.00 and 9.00 pm) to discuss different aspects of writing and to receive feedback on pieces we have written. Our goal is to encourage each others' literary endeavours, as well as to give advice and improve our own writing skills.

We're open to all writers, whether you're just beginning or you are already published. Our group includes all abilities, genres, poets and script writers.

Our meetings consist of storytelling evenings, writing exercises and theme based discussions. We also have established authors and professionals from the writing community as guests to do readings and talks based on their own work.

Visit the Derby Scribes website at www.derbyscribes.co.uk

If you have any questions or queries about Derby Scribes then please feel free to email us at the following address: derbyscribes@googlemail.com

ALT-DEAD

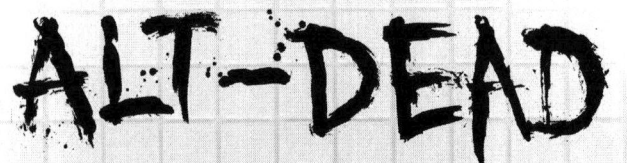

Featuring new fiction from:

Steven Savile & Steve Lockley, Ian Woodhead, Mark West, Dave Jeffery, Stuart Neild, Stephen Bacon, R. J. Gaulding, Zach Black, Katherine Tomlinson, Adrian Chamberlin, Jan Edwards, Stuart Hughes, Richard Farren Barber, Gary McMahon, Stuart Young, Johnny Mains

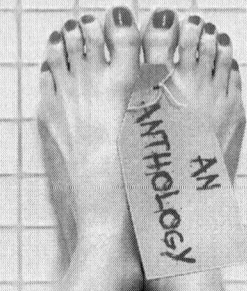

COMING SEPTEMBER 2011

Edited by Peter Mark May

For more information, visit
http://hershamhorrorbooks.webs.com/